SHIFT HAPPENS

SHIFTER LORDS

S.E. BABIN

CHAPTER
One

Two beasts lived inside me. One wanted to heal, the other wanted to kill. The object of my current murderous desires sat on the opposite side of the desk, one ankle crossed over his knee.

He was wearing navy and brick-red argyle socks, which should have been ridiculous, but the well-tailored suit he wore had me in a tongue-tied haze of lust. I focused on those stupid socks and willed myself to come up with a cutting insult, but this fucker smelled amazing and looked like he'd walked out of a high-end suit catalog.

I swear to the gods if he took off his jacket and rolled up that crisp white shirt to show off his muscular forearms, I was going to throw myself at him, à la Scarlett O'Hara style, damn the consequences.

"Moira?"

One of Ethan Flint's dark eyebrows rose. Shit. I'd been silent for too long. Why did all of my wit dry up and turn to ash the moment he turned those midnight eyes on me?

I *was* witty, dammit. I could make a grown man cry with my cutting diatribes and vicious wordplay. It took years of practice to hone my words into sharp daggers, and I usually had to save most of my insults for when I was out of earshot of my BFF Evie. So when I got to use one, I made sure it was a good one.

And yet, when Ethan came around, I was an internal puddle of goo.

"Why are you here?" Not the most cutting of responses, but the only one I could come up with without staring at him like the dolt I currently was.

A smile played at the edge of his lips. "Merely checking to see how you're settling in." He adjusted his watch on his tanned wrist.

Not many men wore watches these days. Not many men were like Ethan these days. Tall, strong, rugged...

If I could punch myself in the face right now, I would.

"I'm fine."

I was most assuredly *not* fine. Eight months ago, all hell had broken loose on Rowan's territory, and I'd watched the man sitting before me die. Not in a metaphorical sense, either. I'd watched a horror show rise up from the earth and tear him apart.

And not only him. I'd watched every single one of the Lords die. Caelan, Thorvin, Ben, Soren, with whom I had my own messed-up history, Rowan, and Ethan here, looking like a total damn snack.

Before that super fucked up period in my history, Ethan was trying to get me to live on his territory for a little while. I'd been resistant, softening only a little when he agreed to do whatever I wanted, provided I went.

Watching him die had shaken something loose inside me. Even knowing it was a mistake, when Fee resurrected him, and I saw him returning to the Ethan I knew, I told him I'd go as soon as we had a contract in place.

And I had.

And now my ass was sitting here designated as the go-between for the fae and Lords for any magical problems they couldn't solve on their own.

A few months ago, my happy ass was clipping flowers and

making bouquets for men with too much money and not enough sense, while my BFF dealt with some pretty heavy magic problems of her own.

Now I helped Evie out part-time and ran a tea shop across the street from hers.

What did this mean? It meant I was majorly unqualified to be any kind of consultant unless you wanted to know if a peony was good enough for an afternoon tea party bouquet.

Answer: Peonies were good for everything, you uncultured swine.

"When a woman says they are 'fine,' it usually means they are anything but." Ethan leaned forward, a hint of his tantalizing scent teasing my sensitive nose. "Are you displeased with your new quarters? Your job duties? Is there something I can assist you with?"

My eyes narrowed. "You were a complete ass about that contract eight months ago. Why be accommodating now?" Unless there was something…

I snorted. "You want something."

Ethan's eyes widened in a gesture of mocking innocence. "I would never."

"You would always. Spit it out, Lord. What is it?"

He sighed. "I've told you a hundred times to call me Ethan."

"Yes, well, I don't call my boss by their first name unless they happen to be my BFF."

His lips thinned. "Must we do this?"

"Do what?" I asked sweetly.

Ethan sat back in his chair and crossed his arms. "I understand you're still pissed about what happened but—"

Even after all this time, his reaction still stung. I squashed those emotions down and locked them in the box I'd made specifically for Ethan. "But nothing. You wanted boundaries. Here they are. You can't put that genie back into the bottle, Lord."

I tossed my pencil down and focused all my attention on him. "Now spill. What do you want?"

Ethan opened his mouth to say something, thought better of it, then snapped it closed.

Probably for the best. He and I got along like oil and water. Shake us up and we mixed in ways where we smothered each other, but leave us alone and we separated, never the twain shall meet.

"Fine," he growled, bending to fish something out of the leather satchel he carried. He slapped a manila folder on my desk. "One of the Lords has an issue. He's requested extra assistance."

I slid the folder over and opened it. A familiar face loomed at me, handsome and mocking.

"I am not working with Soren," I all but snarled.

Ethan sighed. "You do remember your oath of office, correct?"

"Your oath of office was made up on the spot, and you had me in a position where I could not refuse!" I reminded him, the memories of that day rearing up to haunt me.

I was in this sticky position because of this bastard. Granted, he paid me a king's ransom, and I didn't have to work all that much. After Danu and the fae got their asses handed to them and Evie officially took over as the fae queen, things were quiet on that front.

Evie insisted if there were any fae problems, she would address them swiftly. After Danu had killed her mate, Evie went full-throttle goddess and torched every fae left on the battlefield, hundreds, maybe even thousands of fae dead in an instant, turned to dust on the wind.

If they were smart, they would realize Evie was not the person to fuck with. The second she felt the bond go, so had every self-imposed block on her power. My friend changed that day. All of us had.

If someone needed their ass kicked, she no longer gave them the benefit of the doubt. If someone challenged her, she put them down with frightening alacrity. My BFF was over it and would throw down in a heartbeat these days.

I loved this about her, but if Evie thought she frightened people before…

Well, let's just say, Evie was now the monster under the bed for the fae and every supernatural inside this country.

And I was her right-hand woman.

After all, I loved kicking a little ass, so I was all about this new side to my bestie.

A hint of something flickered through Ethan's midnight gaze. Couldn't be guilt. The Lord had no damned soul.

"Regardless, you took the oath and have agreed to look into every issue we need assistance with."

"Soren is an asshole."

He inclined his head. "Yes, all the Lords agree with you, but Soren is in a new territory and has called for aid."

Evie had done the guy a serious solid. Fed up with his former territory, Evie convinced the Lords to cooperate and move Soren from the southern territories up to the lands she'd taken from Donovan. She hadn't given him the entire territory, only a part of Montana and slivers of both North and South Dakota. The former Lord of the South was happy as a pig in shit right now and thought Evie walked on water.

Which…she did, in my opinion, but earning the respect of the Lords was a hard-won battle.

"He barely has anything that could pass for an actual territory." I shoved the folder away. "Is this really important, or am I wasting my time?"

Ethan's lips thinned. "Soren is a young Lord, not as young as Rowan, but close. In his tenure, he has never once called for aid. Can you put your differences aside for a little while and assist him?"

He was making me sound like some petty teenager. I leaned forward. "Do you know why Soren and I don't speak?"

His eyes flickered once more, though his expression remained placid. "I assume you had a relationship. Soren's reputation is both well-documented and well-deserved."

A haze of rage obscured my vision for a split second. How like a man to assume my dislike of another man was because I'd slept with him and he didn't call me the next morning. If he knew anything about me, he'd realize that line of thought was laughable. But I'd seen that flicker in Ethan's eyes, and I knew firsthand how possessive he could be, even when he and I were not involved.

The thought of me sleeping with Soren enraged him, in his typical stoic, hide all emotion, Ethan way.

"Hmm," I said thoughtfully. "Soren pushed for a relationship," I lied through my bright white teeth. "But I was the one who denied him."

Soren had done no such thing. What Soren had done was proposition me repeatedly until I threatened to knock his pretty white teeth down his throat so far, they'd play Chopsticks on their way down.

I looked down at my hands and wrung them together. "He was distraught, and we argued."

Also a lie. Soren was disappointed, but we both knew all he had to do was walk out the door and women would find him like bloodhounds.

Shifters could smell lies, but I was a vampire. When I didn't want to have a heartbeat, I didn't have one. Ethan's eyes narrowed. His nostrils flared as he tried to scent the truth, anger flickering in the depths when he realized he couldn't.

I closed the folder. "Maybe it will be good to see him again. I'm in a much different place than I was back then."

With a shrug, I sighed. "Alright. You win, Ethan. I'll call Soren up and have him grab a room at the Keep." I tilted my head to the side. "Or I suppose there's no harm in staying with me. He's been to my apartment before."

Ethan's nostrils flared again. "I never smelled him there."

I chuckled. "You haven't been back since Danu."

A tiny flicker of glee filled my soul at the blank mask settling over his face. "I've had a few visitors since then."

I smiled and stood, tucking the file into the left desk drawer. "I'll contact Soren once I've had the chance to read everything over. You can pass that on to your little joint council."

Ethan tilted his head up, studying me. I wasn't short, but I'd never loom over the Lord, not even standing while he sat. "No shenanigans, Moira. We can't afford to screw this up."

I rolled my eyes. "First of all, I put the nan in shenanigans. Second, it's Soren. If any shenanigans occur, they're probably his fault. Third, once I take this file, you're out of this, as agreed upon. I don't report to you, nor do I have to give anyone status updates unless you call a council meeting."

I was completely autonomous and there to assess the situation, determine whether it was solvable without violence or other forms of harm, and finally provide a full report to the new joint council. If I could solve the issue while working with the complainant, I would. Otherwise, all I had to do was hand over my findings, and they would come up with a solution. This kept the fae and Lords from each other's throats and accusing the other of hiding potential problems until they spiraled out of control, aka Danu style.

As jobs went, it wasn't terrible. Basically, I got paid to walk in, examine the issue, and either present my findings or, if it was simple enough, resolve it, then walk away with a fat paycheck.

Working with Soren, though, sent a frisson of nerves down my spine. We had not parted well. He made me believe he wanted something real, only for me to realize at the last possible moment he was manipulating me to get into my pants. The moment was forever ingrained in my brain, and I would never forgive him for it.

I rarely trusted anyone, and for him to slide so smoothly underneath my walls told me a hard truth about myself. I so badly wanted someone to see past all that made me who I was and love me for me. While Soren had never confessed love, he made me believe he had very real feelings. For a brief moment in time, he made me feel cherished in a way I never had before.

I only realized it when I confessed my feelings to him, and he hesitated—the briefest, smallest of gestures, but I was part vampire. And then he tried to distract me. I knew men like him. Once upon a time, I ate men like him.

But I couldn't tell Ethan any of it. For many reasons. I would never admit aloud the humiliation I felt, followed by the hurt, followed by my tears and wallowing. Most importantly, the reason neither of us breathed a word about what happened was because the moment I realized what Soren was doing, I tried to kill him.

And came damned close to succeeding.

CHAPTER
Two

E than unfolded his lean form and stood, his expression piercing. "I expect you to call me first."

"Not happening." I walked over to the office door and gestured for him to leave. "Alice has that blend you like. Ask her for a hot tea on your way out."

Ethan didn't budge. He leaned against the doorframe, all muscle and leashed violence. "You're agitated."

"Yes, because there's a stubborn wolf who won't leave me be." I flicked my fingers. "Shoo, dog. Be gone."

His lips twitched. "Dog?"

"Same family."

"Technically, yes, though some domesticated dogs are descended from an extinct species."

"Tea," I said and pointed. "Begone and let me work."

Ethan sighed. "You're still mad."

And therein lay the crux of our issue. I was not mad. Nor was I disappointed. Mostly, I was sad. While I had liked Soren, what I felt for him was nothing compared to what I felt for Ethan.

What was worse? Ethan had repeatedly shown me he wasn't interested. Not only had he shown me, he'd told me point blank he and I would never be in a relationship. Not that I asked him to be in one, or tried to seduce him, or behaved in any way other than appropriately. Ethan was like the boy who cried wolf. He sensed something happening between us and tried to stop it by claiming nothing would ever happen between us.

And yet…he kept showing up. He all but dragged me to his territory, moved me into a small cottage close to his main residence, came over almost every night, and spent more time with me than anyone else in his pack. So I thought he might be coming around.

"I'm not mad." And I wasn't.

"Moira."

I shook my head. "No. You don't get to do this. You've made your feelings perfectly clear, and I've done my best to respect your boundaries. You need to do the same."

Ethan's lips thinned. A thin ring of gold appeared around his irises, one of the few ways I knew he was experiencing high emotion. "Fine," he all but snarled.

"Go get your tea. I'll contact Soren once I acquaint myself with his file."

Ethan's jaw tightened. He left without another word but didn't miss asking Alice for a to-go cup. I was not too proud to admit I watched him walk away the entire time. That man had an ass built for watching.

"Witches," I muttered. "I *hate* witches."

Soren was having trouble with a coven of witches who'd taken up residence on his borrowed lands without permission. I texted Evie to confirm she hadn't authorized a coven to live on her lands, and she promptly denied it. She didn't like witches either.

The real problem wasn't the witches, though. It was the magic they were performing. As a shifter, Soren was naturally resistant to magic. Didn't mean spells couldn't harm him; they certainly could, but it took a lot more power to affect them. If Soren was sensing dark magic seeping through the land around him, whatever spells those witches were working needed to stop. Immediately.

I asked Evie to do a quick health check on the land. She responded a few minutes later, disturbed.

High concentration of bodies in Soren's area, she'd written. *Odd magic. Off, like Danu's but creepier.*

I grimaced. That wasn't good.

Want me to kill them?

I laughed out loud. Knowing Evie these days, she was fifty percent serious.

Not right now. Let me try reasoning with them first.

Okay. I'll kill them when you give me the go-ahead. But this time she put a winky face afterward.

Maybe forty percent serious then.

How's the baby?

Not so little anymore. She's almost walking. Come by the main house. She misses Auntie Moira.

I smiled. Misty was growing up to be a mischievous and adorable baby, and I'd been so busy I hadn't seen her in close to a week. That was forever in baby time.

Is Rowan cooking?

Not after last month's disastrous barbecue. The entire Pack banned him from the kitchen. I'm making lasagna.

I shuddered. Not sure what the fuck Rowan had tossed on the grill that fateful night, but he managed to turn it into a gristled, inedible mess. I once thought a man was genetically incapable of fucking up barbecue. Rowan had proven me wrong.

Even his shifters, who never spoke against their Lord, turned their noses up at it, leaving us scrambling to order enough pizza to feed several hundred ravenous wolves in human form.

Thank the gods. Never let that man hold the tongs again.

Only when he's chasing me around the room!

Eww. Also, yay on the lasagna. I'll be there at 6:30. Save me a seat.

Evie sent a kissy face.

Ever since Danu, Evie's emoji use was out of control. Guess if she couldn't put her feelings into words, a kissy emoji said what she couldn't.

Shaking my head, I flipped another page in Soren's file. Normally, when Ethan handed me a file, he crammed it full of information. This one was strangely light on details, making me wonder who'd put this one together.

Or maybe something else was going on, and Soren was desperate enough to ask for help, while keeping the worst of it to himself. Sounded exactly like something he'd do. I read through the rest of the file, and when I made it to the end, I wondered why the Lord hadn't gone in and taken them all out. Easy enough to do for a Lord, if he caught them unaware.

As much as I was loath to, I'd call him in the morning and see if I could fix this without traveling to his territory. While I wasn't as furious with him anymore, I had no desire to spend time with him. Being polite was okay in small doses and when we were in public. I wasn't sure the urge to claw his face off wouldn't come raging back when I was alone with him for longer than a few minutes.

Alas, something to deal with tomorrow. For now, I had tea to make.

WHEN THE GODS MADE ALICE, they left something out of her DNA. My helper was a shifter, supposedly a wolf, though she was the least wolfish person I'd ever met. If I saw her on the street, I'd peg her as fae. She was petite, maybe four eleven on a good day, and had long, curly blonde hair, so pale it was an odd cross of gold and creamy white. Her eyes were a bright sky blue, and she had a pert, upturned nose. Her lips were shaped in a perfect rosebud, and when she spoke, she had a breathy, Marilynesque tone to her voice.

Everyone underestimated Alice, which always made me laugh. She might look like a wispy fairy, but Alice was whip smart and had a vicious tongue when you crossed her—one she thankfully only used on occasion. The shop could only handle so many one-star reviews, though Rowan was quick to step in when there was a disagreement of some kind with his shifters.

Alice was one of Rowan's, but even he was befuddled by her sometimes.

When I came out of the office, she was leaning against the polished oak of the counter, staring outside. I had no need to stay quiet. Alice's senses were sharp and honed. She'd smell me first before she heard my footsteps.

"I'm surprised you haven't hog-tied that man and carried him to your lair yet."

That was Alice. You never knew what she was going to say.

Her hair was tied in a wild, loose bun atop her head and secured with a cute apple clip, made by one of the artisans in town.

"A one-bedroom apartment is not a lair, and I don't think Ethan could relinquish control long enough to allow someone to tie him up. Even if it's for fun."

Alice grinned. "Well, I think you should try. Maybe if you ask nicely, he'll come around."

I shook my head. She knew something was up between the other Lord and me and teased me every time he came around. Which was too damn much. Maybe I could have Rowan ban him.

"I have zero desire to tie anyone up these days." Not strictly true, but Alice and I weren't besties. I'd consider her a friend, but she was a shifter. Odds were good if I confided in her, word would get back to Rowan.

Shifter clans were tight, and their gossip lines were hot as a midnight bonfire during a full moon.

Her lips pursed. "Liar." She tapped the side of her nose. "If you're worried about me chatting with the other wolves, don't be. They're convinced I'm a fae changeling, switched at birth."

Alice rolled her eyes. "Never mind they see me shift all the time." Her tone was level, but her heartbeat was faster than normal. "I'm looking for a place outside of the Keep, but I have to convince Rowan first."

All the Lords wanted their people to live on site at the Keep, Rowan being no exception. Shifters tended to be more volatile as a general rule, and they were easier to bring under control when they lived in close proximity to their Lord. He'd made exceptions to this rule before, but those were for older, much more established shifters.

I wouldn't get involved, but I could help ease her way a little. "If I were you, I'd come up with a strong argument on why it would benefit both you and the Pack to move off-site. Rowan appreciates a well thought out plan. Could move the needle a little."

To her credit, Alice didn't ask me to use my friendship with Evie to influence Rowan. We'd worked together a while now, long enough for her to know I wouldn't. Being BFFs with the fae queen and the Lady of the territory was a little weird. To me, she was just Evie.

To everyone else, she was an almost godlike figure. Which, to be fair, technically she was. Evie = goddess = wife to Rowan = Emberwood's Lady. Rowan, on the other hand, was both Lord and the fae king. They were my besties, but they were also the most powerful couple in the entire United States.

Weird to think about since Evie once arm wrestled a shifter inside a bar and won. The memory made me smile. Man, I loved that bitch.

"Like a PowerPoint?" Alice asked, staring at me like I had two heads.

"The more detailed the better. But maybe go for Canva. More graphics and ways to wow him."

Alice's brow furrowed, but she nodded. "Huh. Like a real-life boardroom proposal."

"Couldn't hurt. I can guarantee you'd be the first shifter to throw a slideshow his way."

Alice grinned. "Sold. I'll work on something this week and try to get on his schedule for next week."

Now that was something I could help with. I wouldn't sway his decision, but I could smooth the way a bit. "I'll mention to Evie you want a meeting. She'll make it happen."

Her expression brightened. "Thanks, Moira!"

She noted my purse and the canvas bag I held. "Leaving early?"

"A little bit, but you've got me for another couple of hours. Tell me what I can do to help out." I tucked my things under the register and tied an apron on.

Always happy for an extra pair of hands, Alice shoved a list at me. "If we get everything checked off, we won't have to come in early tomorrow."

"Then let's get busy!"

Soon, the scent of Earl Grey and roasted Oolong filled the air, and my brain settled into a relaxing rhythm. I'd worry about Ethan and Soren tomorrow.

For the rest of the day, all I had to worry about was tea.

CHAPTER
Three

Going back to work the next morning felt a lot better after spending time with my bestie and the Pack's adopted Chimera baby. I cherished all the sweet snuggles and good food Evie had all but stuffed in my face. But now, it was time to face the real world once more.

I had a Lord I needed to talk to.

Soren answered on the second ring. "Moira?"

The surprise in his voice made me chuckle. After the way we parted, I was the last person he expected to hear from.

"Hello, Lord."

He sighed. "Moira. It's Soren."

"Mmm. Not today. I'm contacting you about the request for help you placed with the junior council."

He swore under his breath. "It came to you?"

"Do you think I'd be calling you otherwise?" I asked dryly.

He let out a short laugh. "Yeah. Probably not." Soren paused. "Shit. Okay. Sorry about that. I thought they'd send in someone else."

"There is no one else. I am the only consultant for the junior council at this time. Until they give it a fancier, capitalized name and get a budget, you're stuck with me."

"Those rich assholes have all the money in the world."

"Yes," I agreed. "Now, looks like you have some witches that need to be dealt with?"

"I know what you're thinking. You're wondering why I haven't chased them out."

"A little, yes. Would you like to explain?"

"Their wards burn."

I paused. A lot of shifters could bypass wards with no real harm. Trickier when they were fae wards, but after Evie became queen, she shut down that kind of cooperation with an iron fist. She wasn't against cooperation between our kind, only made it clear that the shit Marnie and Twyla had done while working with the fae would end in a death sentence.

Since that time, everyone's been a lot more wary in their behavior.

"Burn how?"

Soren hesitated. "I can't break through them. Neither can the mages."

Curious. "Did the mages say anything else about them? Could they be fae made?"

"They would have said something if they were. The Head Mage said he'd never seen the likes of them."

Hmm. "Can you catch any of the witches unaware outside their wards?"

I could almost hear Soren's teeth gnashing. "No." His voice had taken on a deep rumble.

"It's like they're ghosts. One minute, they're right where I can see them. The next, they've disappeared into thin air."

"As if by magic?" I said helpfully.

"Moira. Make fun if you want, but there's something disturbing going on here."

I sat back in my chair and tilted my face up to the ceiling. "Hmm. Alright. I'll bite. Why your territory? Why you?"

"I've never dealt with witches in my entire life. As far as I know, I've never pissed any of them off, and I've certainly never frequented their shops."

"Yes, well, witches are women, Soren. The more important question is, have you ever pretended to love one, slept with her, and dumped or ghosted her the next morning?"

The tense silence told me everything I needed to know.

I let out a soft huff of laughter. "You beautiful idiot."

"Suppose I have—"

"We both know there's no supposing about it, Soren. Of all the people you could have done something like that to, you did it to a witch?" I shook my head. "You're lucky you haven't woken up with your balls outside your body."

"Thanks," Soren drawled.

"I'm serious. Witches are not known for being kind to men who abuse them."

He sucked in a breath. "I did not abuse anyone!"

I clicked my tongue. "Men. So handsome. So strong. So. Terribly. Dumb. Abuse is not limited to physical harm, Soren. Let me break this down in a semi-academic way. What you did to her was sexual coercion by deception, sometimes called rape by deception."

"Moira! Fucking—"

"Stop talking, Soren."

He sucked in a breath and shut up.

"Good boy. Now, sexual coercion by deception is the term used when someone, regardless of gender, consents to sexual intercourse because the other party has issued false statements, perceptions, or participated in false actions in order to get them to agree to such an act. Would the witch have consented if you hadn't love-bombed her with gifts, false promises, and/or the illusion of catching feelings?"

Soren's silence said it all.

"I should leave you there to rot," I said quietly.

"Do it, then, since you think I'm such a horrible person."

I laughed. "Uh uh. You don't get to passive-aggressively try to turn this back on me. I'm not the one out there promising the moon to land women."

I shook my head. "The crazy thing is, you don't have to do any such thing. You're handsome, wealthy, and have more power than 99% of the men in this country. Getting women to like you wouldn't be an issue. But you like a challenge, and when things aren't working out, you resort to deception so you can win."

And just like that, it clicked. "Huh," I said aloud, figuring something out about Soren I'm sure he'd never want anyone else to know.

The handsome Lord wanted to be loved, was desperate for it, in fact, but couldn't break his cycle of wanting to be adored. That wasn't real life. Love was heat and fire and yearning, but it eventually banked into something warm and cozy. Soren had never stuck around for the warm and cozy.

He always wanted to be on fire.

"I want you to try this," I said. "Is this witch or witches you did this to living inside that coven?"

"Yes."

"Then I want you to go there and apologize."

"Godsdammit, Moira. An *apology*? You think that would work with a bunch of furious coven members?"

"You have no idea how far a sincere apology could go, Soren. Maybe give it a try for once in your life. And for fuck's sake, maybe bring flowers. Hell, show up with a truckload of money. I dunno. Just don't be an insufferable dick about it."

His heavy sigh delighted me. "And if they fry me?"

"I suggest you run very fast when you see the magic coming."

Soren's blustering just as I hung up the phone made me snicker.

What an asshole.

THE INEVITABLE ASS chewing came a few hours later.

I held the phone up to my ear and didn't bother to say a word.

"Godsdammit, Moira! You told a Lord to apologize? What the fuck kind of advice is that?"

"Hello, Ethan. I hadn't heard from you in almost twenty-four hours and was wondering if you'd perhaps fallen into a pit."

"Cut this shit, Moira. What kind of bullshit advice is that?"

All amusement dropped from my voice. "It's good advice," I snapped. "Advice more men should listen to when they do something as profoundly fucking stupid as Soren did."

Ethan paused.

"Ha. I should have known that asshole wouldn't tell you. He needs to apologize, Ethan, because he lured those witches to bed with false promises, and they're understandably a little pissed about it!"

He sighed. "Moira, that's the age old—"

I closed my eyes for a brief second. "Don't you *dare* say something insane like boys will be boys. You think Evie didn't like you when you first met her? I will legit come to where you are and bite your fucking face off and leave it on the Council's desk for the waitstaff to use as a doily if you finish that thought."

Ethan's snort of laughter came over the line. "Fair enough. You win. Soren issues an apology—"

"A *sincere* apology, Ethan. None of his *look at me, I'm so handsome and innocent* bullshit Soren is famous for pulling. The witches will see right through him. And listen, I'm not saying this will work. Odds are good it won't. But first, he owes them an apology. Soren is a dickhead, and his actions have probably caught up to him. It's worth a try, at least."

Ethan fell silent for a long moment. So long, I cleared my throat. "Are you still there?"

When he spoke, his voice had turned to gravel. "Is there a reason you're so adamant about this? Does Soren owe you a similar apology?"

"Neither here nor there. I'm packing up this evening and plan to head into Soren's territory tomorrow. I should have a report in the next seventy-two hours."

"Do you really need to go into his territory?"

"If you'd like this solved, yes, I do."

"Are you going to answer my question?"

"I just did."

"You know which question," Ethan growled.

"Seventy-two hours. Also, I want a raise."

"You've been on the job for less than a year!" Ethan sputtered. "And we're paying you an ungodly sum!"

"Yes, and I noticed you haven't hired anyone else. I didn't sign up to do things like deal with Soren's overactive dick problems."

Ethan snorted. "Moira, can you please tone it down? Soren is a Lord."

"I don't see what that has to do with me. And we both know I'm right. I'm surprised that thing hasn't turned to dust and fallen right off. He's definitely got a BIFL deal out of his unit."

I could almost see the wheels turning in Ethan's head. He didn't want to ask, but he couldn't help himself. "BIFL?" he repeated.

"Yup. Buy it for life. That thing has taken a licking and keeps on ticking."

"For the gods' sake, Moira!" Ethan blustered.

I laughed and hung up the phone.

That bastard, Ethan, must have warned Soren I was coming. He stood at the edge of the property line, leaning against a massive oak tree, looking every bit as delicious as he did the last time I saw him.

He was taller than the other Lords, six four if I had to guess. Messy chestnut-colored hair fell over his face, a touch longer than I was used to seeing on him, and startling blue eyes topped off his handsome countenance. When Soren really looked at you, it felt like he was staring right at your soul.

Who was I kidding? Soren had one good thing working for him. He was a handsome bastard. The rest I could take or leave.

"Moira," he said, those blue eyes somber as he watched me step over the territory line. Evie had the entire territory under her control and warded to the gills. No reason to ward this part of the area, even though Rowan had asked her to.

I thought he was pushing his luck, but Evie just sighed. "He's a Lord. They're all used to getting what they want." Her eyes sparkled as she added, "So it's a lot more fun to tell them no now."

Evie was no longer the small-town florist she only ever

wanted to be. Now she could close her eyes and kick all their asses with one finger behind her back and not feel bad about it. If she told Soren no, the Lord was smart enough to cut his losses while he was ahead. After all, she'd given him brand new territory with very little responsibility.

"Soren." I inclined my head. "You're looking well."

His lips thinned at the subtle dig. The last time we'd seen each other, I'd almost clawed his eyes out as I screamed, "*All you have going for you is a pretty face because there's not a goddamn speck of intellect in your unused head cavity!*"

Yeah. I was a little pissed that night. Sue me.

He turned and started walking, gesturing for me to follow. "The house is about a quarter mile up. I set up a room for you."

I stared at him and let out a surprised laugh. "I'm not staying at the Keep."

His shoulders stiffened. "There's no reason not to stay with me."

"There's every reason," I retorted. "The most important being if the witches try to burn your house down, my ass is not dying with you."

Soren sighed. "You're worse than Evie," he muttered. "So much worse."

"Took you all long enough to see it," I said sweetly.

"At least come up to the house so I can feed you. I'll have one of my people take you to a hotel as soon as you're ready." He looked over his shoulder. "The closest hotel is forty-five minutes away."

Nice try. Soren was always looking for an angle. "I made reservations earlier."

He'd chosen the most remote part of the territory to host his watered-down Keep. Eighty percent of his people elected to stay behind when he left, and a permanent Lord had yet to be installed in his old region. Garrett refused the job, and Pax, the only other viable choice, wasn't quite ready.

Even if he was, I doubted he'd take it. Evie had all but stolen Pax when she visited Ben's territory a few months ago. He'd been enamored with her the moment they met, and his fascination showed no signs of slowing down.

Rowan was more bemused than anything. Pax was a perfect gentleman and treated her exactly how a shifter would treat the Lady of his territory, but there was something…not off about him, more odd. Plus, he smelled a little funny. Not in a bad way, more in a not-exactly-pure-shifter kind of way.

Darios, the other potentially viable choice, had taken off to parts unknown after seeing some of the insanity revolving around Evie and the Lords. No one had seen him since. Whether he was alive or plotting world domination or had taken to plunking his head in the sand like an ostrich was anyone's guess.

"And if I need you right away?" Soren asked.

I smiled. "I'll respond accordingly, while also keeping in mind you're a big boy and can run real fast."

Soren sighed and kept walking. Occasionally, he turned to ensure I was still following, but we spent most of the walk in silence.

Fine by me. I said everything I needed to say to him that fateful night.

We came upon a large white house with an adorable wrap-around porch. Land dotted with colorful wildflowers spread as far as the eye could see. White smoke piped from the chimney. The elevation was higher here, lending a nip to the slight breeze ruffling our hair. I inhaled fresh, cool air and felt my shoulders settle.

Soren looked good here. He shoved his hands in his pockets and trudged up the driveway, not a soul coming out to greet him. Unusual, but Soren had an odd relationship with his people. Now that he was down to a skeleton crew, I was sure they were stretched to max capacity.

We went up the porch steps, the creak of old wood sending a

memory rushing through my brain of quieter, simpler times. I brushed the thoughts away and centered myself firmly in the present. While I had good memories, most were filled with blood and despair.

If I didn't keep myself grounded in the present, I felt like I would drown in the pain of my past.

There was an old rocking chair with a colorful blanket slung across the back on the right side of the porch and a small wooden table parked beside it. A whiskey bottle and rocks glass sat on top of the scarred surface. Surprisingly, someone had planted a large circular pot of colorful flowers and totally nailed the thriller, filler, spiller adage. A spiky plant with brilliant orange blooms loomed several inches high, surrounded by a shorter, glossy-leafed plant with creamy white blooms. The edges of the pot spilled over with what looked to be mounding petunias in a medley of bright colors.

"Did you plant those?" I asked as I came up behind him.

Soren glanced at the pot. "I did." He rubbed the back of his neck as if embarrassed. "This place is wonderful, but it's not like my old territory. I'd forgotten how remote the wilderness could be."

A piece of the ice surrounding my heart cracked. "You got lonely."

His smile was sheepish. "And bored. There's a great nursery a few miles up the road with supplies. In my spare time, I'm building a greenhouse at the back of the property."

I eyed him. "Aren't you worried about putting anything permanent here if Evie yanks her property back?"

Soren shrugged. "I wasn't worried until you so aptly pointed out my fuck up with the witches." He pulled a chair from the opposite side of the porch and brought it close to the rocking chair. "Have a seat. I'll bring out some of that lavender lemonade you like."

I glared at him, but Soren ignored me and headed inside.

The bastard knew I liked that lemonade. He was trying to catch me off guard.

Wasn't going to happen. I'd allowed it once and once was more than enough for me.

He came back out with a glass pitcher of purple lemonade and two glasses. Once he poured us both a glass, he sat in the rocking chair and looked out at the property.

"This place really is incredible," he mused. "Louisiana is flat and hot as hell."

Soren sighed and shook his head. "I had to go out and buy a whole new wardrobe."

"Oh noes," I said softly.

Soren snorted. "Are you ever not an asshole, Moira?"

I shrugged and sipped my lemonade. "Can't rightly say. It's been so long, I can't quite remember a time when I've been less witty."

Soren's scent was unique but familiar. All the Lords' scents held a tinge of the wild. Ethan reminded me of crisp snow and pine, mixed with something I couldn't quite put my finger on. Sometimes his scent changed, but he always remained just Ethan.

To me, Soren smelled like sin and silken sheets, a hint of cinnamon, and a touch of pine. Intoxicating until you got to know the bastard. Male models were considered the standard of beauty by many people. Soren did not look like a model. He looked like *more*. I always found describing him difficult. He was beautiful, the perfect package wrapped up in physical perfection and wit.

I always thought that regardless of what women said out loud, there was something about a man's physical prowess that revved our engines, provided they preferred the male sex. Even if they didn't, sometimes masculinity smacked you right in the face, and even the staunchest disbelievers had to admit that yeah, sometimes someone just *had* it.

Like Henry Cavill. The United Kingdom's greatest gift to the world, minus the guillotine. And for those who think the French invented that wonderful piece of chop-chop machinery, think again. In fact, there was a wonderful tradition that claimed if a condemned person could get their head out of the contraption once the blade started to fall, their sentence would be commuted, provided they never returned.

"Moira!"

I blinked, jerked from my internal session on fun facts about guillotines. "What?"

He was staring at me with something akin to awe. "I swear. I know vampires can't have ADD, but your mind is like a squirrel on a treadmill sometimes."

"Piss off, Soren. Maybe it's just the company."

The Lord chuckled.

Yeah. He was a handsome bastard, alright. If he weren't such a self-absorbed dickhead, he'd be a real force to reckon with. But Soren was far too busy admiring his muscles in the mirror to worry about little things like oh…let's see, witches plotting his permanent demise.

He poured himself another glass of lemonade and topped mine off. "What were you thinking about?"

"Guillotines," I said with a sweet smile.

Soren's brow furrowed. "I can't help but think you're serious."

"I am."

A male appeared in the distance, tall and lean, like most shifters, but this one had a palpable air of power about him. "Is that your replacement if the witches take you out?" I murmured.

"Fucking hell, Moira."

I grinned. "He's pretty, too."

Soren's sigh was one for the ages. "Seth is dangerous as hell."

"Hmm. So am I."

The look he sent my way this time was considering. "Yes," he murmured after a moment. "I suppose you are."

When Seth came close enough, I gave him a good once over. Evie mentioned him after she'd returned from visiting Soren before all the shit with Danu. I remembered our conversation because she mentioned Seth was dangerous. Not that he looked dangerous (because he did) or sounded dangerous, but that he was dangerous. He'd made no move to attack her, but something inside Evie recognized the predator living inside of him.

I wondered how long Seth spent in his wolf form and if he hadn't come back quite the same when he finally regained his human form.

"You keep staring at me like that, and we'll find a good spot away from here to let you see the rest of me."

Oh Jaysus, Mary, and Josephine. His southern drawl was sweet, molten gold honey, pouring over my skin like warm sunshine.

I took another sip of my lemonade. "You keep talking like that, and I might just let you."

"For fuck's sake," Soren muttered.

"I'm Moira."

His gaze flicked to Soren, a question in his eyes. Ah. He'd heard of me before. The shifter inclined his head. "Seth. Soren's Second."

"Nice to meet you."

"Likewise." He pulled up another chair and set it to face us. "I'm surprised not to be pulling you two off each other."

Soren closed his eyes.

"Do you mean like strangling each other or…?"

"Exactly that. Heard Soren really screwed the pooch with you."

I let out a bark of laughter. "You could say that. Instead of learning his lesson, he did it again."

Soren squeezed the space between his brows.

Seth grinned. "In his defense, he pissed off the witches before he acted like an idiot with you."

"Ah. Well then, I think it's safe to say we might have more than just the witches trying to kill him soon."

"I like her," Seth pronounced. "The little goddess was pretty but wary. This one has claws."

"Evie keeps her claws sheathed until she has them buried in your throat." I shrugged. "Mine are always out."

"Fair enough."

I filled my glass of lemonade and handed it over. Shifters didn't care about germs, and he gratefully took my offering.

"You're not here to help him with the witches, are you?" Seth sent a dubious look in Soren's direction.

"I am right here," he growled. "And yes, that is what she's here for."

Seth let out a low whistle and looked at me. "Who'd you piss off?"

Sure felt like I'd angered the gods. "Unfortunately, I'm the only consultant on their new council. When Soren asked the Lords for help, they sent me."

Seth winced. "Alright. I'll bite. What's the first step we should take in getting them out of the territory? Their wards have proven invincible. We can't cross them, and our mages assure us they are not fae made."

I leaned forward. "Yes. I've come up with a great plan."

Soren scrubbed a hand over his face. "Moira."

Seth's eyes lit up. "Oh? What do we need to do?"

A vicious grin touched my lips. "First, Soren needs to apologize to them for being a man whore."

Seth blinked once. Twice. A third time. His lips twitched just as realization struck. "Sonofabitch, Soren. You got involved with a witch?"

I shook my head and put on my best somber expression. "No. Witches. Plural. He hasn't admitted to the exact number, but there are thirteen witches in the coven, so I'm sure Soren put on a heroic effort to get to know each of them."

"Godsdammit, Moira," Soren growled. "I did *not* sleep with an entire coven!"

Seth burst out laughing. "Half?"

The Second and I grinned at each other. I liked this guy. "You and I are going to have fun together."

He winked. "Looking forward to working together on Soren's Great Apology World Tour."

"Fuckers," Soren said as he stood up and flung his front door open. He disappeared inside, the door slamming behind him.

"Aww. Poor wittle Lord got his feelings hurt," I said in a baby voice.

Seth chuckled. "Fun indeed, Moira."

CHAPTER
Five

"You're bringing a wagon?" I asked in disbelief.

Soren threw his hands in the air. "You told me to get flowers! How the hell was I supposed to bring them?"

I counted the vases. "Soren. There are…"

"Eight," Seth said, one eyebrow rising.

"Eight," I repeated flatly. "You slept with *eight* witches in the same coven." I couldn't even make it a question. The proof was in the numerous, over-the-top bouquets Evie would hate. Could you really say you were sorry with a wagon full of flowers meant for different women who lived together after your dick had been in most of them?

We were *so* screwed. Soren was definitely dying soon.

"Dude." Seth shoved his hands through his hair. "I was joking about half the witches. I thought three at absolute most. And even then, I was judging you a little. But eight?" He blew out a long breath. "Fucking hell. You really are a man whore."

Soren kicked the wagon's tire, sending all the vases rattling. "Alright. That's enough!" A ring of gold outlined his irises. "Look. I get it. I fucked up."

I scratched my nose. "And sideways and missionary and—"

"MOIRA!"

Seth coughed to cover up his laugh.

I put my hands over my mouth so I would stop talking. Honestly, if Soren died, he kinda deserved it. Not even the gods would have sympathy for someone who'd literally fucked himself to death. Witches were not known to be kind and benevolent. I mean, sure, there were white witches. Magic was magic was magic, right?

The intent was in the spell caster. Humans, like many paranormals, were easily corruptible. If you threw riches or women or their heart's desire at them, a lot would go to the dark side.

But when you had magic on your side? Why walk on the right side of the law when you could get everything you wanted with very little effort?

For whatever reason, Soren had fooled them all with his honeyed tongue and pretty eyes. Hell, he'd almost fooled me, but I couldn't help feeling a little smug about escaping his clutches.

I would have been just another notch on his bedpost, and that, as much as I hated to admit, would have hurt me. As it was, I walked out of there that night feeling like my heart was breaking, even knowing I wasn't in love with him.

"How long ago was this?" I asked.

Soren tilted his head up to the sky and squinted.

"Gods," I muttered. "Are you really sorting through your trysts right now?"

"Two years ago, give or take a few months," he finally said, ignoring my question.

"I bet they followed you here from New Orleans, which is good for you. Odds are good I wouldn't have found them had you stayed in your old territory. Every inch of that place is saturated with magic. Even with my sensitive nose, they'd be ghosts."

I put my hands on my hips and thought about our next steps. Knowing what I knew now, an apology seemed like a stupid plan. "How'd you figure out they were here?"

"By accident," he admitted. "I was out exploring and stumbled upon the scent of magic. When I followed it back, I found them."

"Do they have a house?"

Soren nodded.

"Hmm. Send me the location. I'll send it to Evie so she can track down who it belongs to."

Seth was still staring at the flowers in horror. "Knowing what we know now, I'm not sure you should deliver these."

"Agreed."

Soren's eyes glowed. He was pissed. "Are you serious? Do you know how much these cost?"

"Yes, well, consider this a down payment for us saving your sorry ass," I growled. "No one would expect *eight* witches, Soren. That's the Cirque du Soleil of dick waving, dude. A lot of people haven't even had eight partners!"

Seth and Soren's attention snapped to me.

My cheeks heated. "If you ask, I will claw both of you."

Seth held his hands up and looked away, but Soren's eyes narrowed as if debating whether it'd be worth it.

My claws slid from the edges of my fingernails, sharp and lethal. Soren's gaze drifted down to my hands, amusement twinkling in his eyes. "Keep your secrets, Moira."

"Oh, I will," I assured him, keeping my claws out a little while longer in case he wanted to keep testing me. Soren was not my Lord, nor did I owe him deference. My position afforded me the autonomy to make decisions that benefited the good of the whole, not the good of the Lords.

Being professional felt impossible when all I wanted to do was punch him in the face. We had a bad history together, and the last thing I wanted was to spend any more time with him than I had to.

Seth cleared his throat. "Hate to bring the party down, but are we doing anything about this tonight? If not..." He rubbed the back of his neck. "Wouldn't mind hitting the town."

"You got eight on the line?" I drawled.

Seth snorted. "Shit. Not a chance. No one in their right mind would keep two women dangling, much less eight."

He didn't have to look at Soren to let him know he was judging the hell out of him.

Soren sighed. "Moira? Up to you."

"Yeah. Ditch the flowers." I eyed what he was wearing. "Put on something a little less douchey."

Seth turned to hide his grin. He had to be loving this. Few people could speak to their Lords like I did, and it was probably nice to hear Soren dressed down a bit for idiotic behavior.

The Lords, no matter how much they liked to pretend, were not omnipotent.

Soren frowned and glanced down at himself. "This is not douchey."

I pointed to his pants. "Wool trousers that cost more than my earrings. Italian leather loafers." I tilted my head and studied his pullover sweater. "Merino wool, if I had to guess, the undershirt a blend of silk and cashmere or cashmere and cotton. Can't quite tell."

I pointed to his wrist. "Thousand-dollar watch." The ring he wore on his right hand. "At least 14k gold. Looks hand-hammered." Then his belt. "Designer. Italian-made."

At his astonished look, I shrugged. "I bet that whatever you have underneath all of that is just as expensive, correct?"

Soren swore and turned on his heel to stomp inside.

"Douchey?" Seth asked. He reached for the pitcher and poured himself another glass.

"He looks like the son of an Italian fashion magnate, and we're in frigging Montana."

Seth, on the other hand, looked like he belonged here. His uniform of the day was a pair of old, faded blue jeans, dusty boots, and a button-down denim shirt. No hat, but it wasn't too cold today. "Old habits die hard."

He slid a glance my way. "So, what's your deal?"

"My deal?"

"Yeah. You and Soren. I know you two aren't dating."

"No," I said slowly. "There is no deal. I'm here because I'm the only one available. Soren conveniently left out he was involved with all of the witches he's trying to cast out, so that's definitely going in the report. If we can solve this tonight, we can go home."

"But something happened there."

"You know something. I can tell."

He lifted a powerful shoulder in a shrug. "We've all heard of you. Evie's best friend. A vampire that's not quite a vampire."

"Don't bullshit me. Soren said something."

A slow smile curved his lips. "Said you were off limits." He paused. "Are you?"

Amusement trickled through me. "How about we get through this bullshit first, alright?"

Soren stomped back out, looking a lot more acclimated to the place he lived in.

Seth chuckled. "Fair enough."

I gave the Lord a once-over. Blue jeans, dark wash, and obviously new, leather boots—no dust. And another Merino pullover. Not perfect but better. Soren always looked yummy. There was just no getting around it. At least now he looked less boardroom and more upper-class country club.

"How far away are the witches?" I asked.

Soren threw his hands up. "You're not going to say anything?"

"Fishing for compliments is unattractive," I said primly.

Seth snickered.

Soren's dark glare made my lips twitch. "Several miles. We'll need an ATV."

"Too much noise. Can we run it?"

Seth's eyebrows flicked up. "Can you match us in speed?"

"Guess we'll find out, won't we?"

Soren checked his watch—this one more sedate with a leather band. "Sunset will be here in an hour or so. Should we go in daylight?"

"No. I'll need a place in the shadows in case things go awry and I need to step in."

Soren rolled his eyes. "I don't need protection."

"If you didn't, you wouldn't have sent your plea to the junior council."

"Moira," he growled.

"I'm here, and this is my show, so we're doing it my way. Seth can go in with you and stand as your Second, but I plan to stay downwind. Never underestimate a witch, Soren. That's how you end up dead."

And I would know. A shiver rolled through me as best forgotten memories tried to surface. I kept my face blank and shoved them down. "Got any food in that house?"

Soren flicked his fingers at the door. "There's a cold bag on the hook by the fridge. Pack what you think we'll need."

"I'll help," Seth said, starting to rise.

"No," Soren said quickly. "I need you out here. Moira's fine to go inside."

Obviously, Soren wanted to talk about me, but I didn't care. "Have fun, boys," I said as I stood and went inside.

I peeked over my shoulder to see Soren stalking toward Seth, death in his eyes.

Another day. Another Lord drama.

CHAPTER

Six

SOREN

"Does she know?" Seth asked, staring at the space Moira had just vacated.

"Hard to say." I had about a hundred emotions roaring through me, confusing and annoying, and I wasn't sure how to handle any of them.

"How long was she there?"

"A few months, I think. She doesn't tell me anything anymore."

Seth scratched his chin. "Should we tell her?"

I scoffed. "Fuck no. Moira is salty on a good day. Tell her something like that, and she's bound to kill the messenger."

Seth gave me a look. "Yeah, dude. Not sure about that. I think she just hates you. Not me."

True, but I wasn't about to admit it to the asshole. Seth was a friend, and I trusted him, but we'd never bonded in the way some Lords did with their Seconds.

Mine tended to ooze disapproval at some of my admittedly poor decisions involving women. And he was looking at Moira in a way that made me want to rip his face off.

But yes, this current thing was a little disturbing.

As if summoned from the fiery pits of hell, my cell rang,

Ethan's name flashing on the screen when I dug it out of my pocket.

Seth grimaced. "She told him."

"She had to. Her position requires her to keep the other Lords informed, and she's always taken her duties seriously." Moira was a lot of things, but I never doubted her dedication to whatever duties she was assigned or loyalty to those she cared about. Unfortunately, I no longer fit into the second category.

"You could have asked her nicely to delay the inevitable." The bastard laughed. We both knew Moira was ill-inclined to do anything to help me out.

The phone kept ringing.

"Might want to answer. He's not a Lord I want to be on the bad side of."

My lips compressed. Seth was right. "Fuck," I snarled and pressed the answer button.

"EIGHT WOMEN?" Ethan roared into the phone. "ARE YOU INSANE?"

Letting him see me vulnerable was not an option. Correction. It was never an option. Not if I wanted to be respected. "Yes, well," I drawled. "I have been very busy these days."

Seth winced and stood, giving me the privacy I wasn't sure I wanted.

"You idiot," he snarled. "And I sent Moira of all people?"

"I didn't ask for her." True. I had no idea this would get smacked down to her level, though I suppose I should have. A Lord should be able to handle a small coven of witches. But these were not regular witches. Something was off about all of them. Like many shifters, I didn't care for witches.

I did, however, love women. Obviously. And a witch was a woman. I wasn't there for their magic.

"What on earth possessed you to tangle with an entire coven?" The anger was mostly gone from Ethan's voice. He just sounded tired.

"Not an entire coven. Give me some credit."

"Drop the bullshit playboy act, Soren. You can get away with that shit around the other Lords, but I've known you far too long. I see under that veneer of designer clothing and perfect hair to the man underneath."

I went still. No one saw anything I didn't want them to see. Ethan was bluffing.

"You didn't give us all the information. If there's magic around that place a Lord can't walk through, you're dealing with more than witches."

"I don't sense anything else."

"Yes, well, considering you're the reason we're in this pickle now, forgive me if I don't take your judgment at face value."

Rage flickered around the edges of my skin. I took a deep, silent breath and held it for a moment before slowly releasing it. "This happened a couple of years ago. Before Moira."

Ethan said nothing for a long moment. "And after her?"

I remembered the way her face looked when she realized what I was doing, the pain in her stunning dark eyes as they widened with horror. Something inside me broke that night, and I hadn't found all the pieces to put myself back together again.

"Does it matter?"

"Yes, it fucking matters," Ethan snarled. "How many more times are we going to have to clean up your messes because you couldn't keep your dick in your pants?"

I resisted the urge to snarl back. Ethan knew nothing about me. Yes, I'd made a huge mistake. I'd made plenty of those over the years. Part of the reason I longed to leave Louisiana was because of those mistakes. Part of it was because of what I'd done to Moira.

I'd done the same thing many times, and most chalked it up to normal male behavior, but those were the women who lived that life—the ones doing the same thing I was. We dressed up in our best, went out on the town, and hoped to find someone to sink into to numb the pain, and while we went into it hopeful, all of us knew deep in our hearts it wouldn't be anything more than a moment in time. Until the next time we went out and repeated the cycle over and over again for eternity.

Moira was different. She'd genuinely cared about me, and I realized it far too late to course correct. Worse, she'd believed the words I'd repeated to dozens, maybe hundreds, of women before her. I thought she was like me, but I'd been so very wrong.

Moira wasn't like anyone I'd ever known before, and I'd screwed things up so profoundly, she barely looked me in the eye anymore. I wasn't used to the constant guilt gnawing in my gut. Every time I looked at her, I wanted to throw myself to my knees and beg her forgiveness, but she didn't want it. No, Moira wanted something far worse.

She wanted me to be a better man.

"That won't be a problem," I responded.

"I don't believe for one moment you've stopped dipping your wick into the overflowing honey pot of nightclubs and bars," Ethan said dryly. "So why should I believe you?"

"I haven't slept with a single woman since the fallout with Moira!" I snapped.

Silence fell over the line, the crackle of tension silent but there. Like me, Moira had tangled Ethan up. Whatever was between them was none of my business, but Ethan needed to know to tread lightly with her.

"Is that right?" Ethan mused, an odd note in his voice. "Are you in love with her?"

"Goddammit, Ethan. Should you be asking yourself the same question?"

"Watch yourself, Soren."

"Your scent is all over her."

"She spent months at my Keep." A thin note of displeasure laced his tone.

"No, Ethan." He had to know. Or he'd buried his head so far in the sand he couldn't smell a thing. "Your scent is ingrained in her. Every shifter in a mile radius senses it."

Silence on the line.

"Is there a reason you're pointing this out?" His voice held a touch of a growl. "Do you wish to stake your own claim?"

Ethan's amusement pissed me off.

"I don't know what happened between you two, but Moira can barely hide her disdain when your name is mentioned."

The barb hit true. Guilt and loathing warred inside me, but I wouldn't give the bastard the satisfaction of knowing. "Then it sounds like I have a lot of making up to do. Eventually your scent will fade. We both know you won't go forward with a mating bond, even if this is the beginning of one."

I couldn't quite tell. His scent was prevalent, yes, but Moira's magic seemed ever changing. If there was a mating bond, it hadn't formed. There was definitely something there, but nothing I'd seen before.

Regardless, Ethan's scent lingering inside her skin was an obvious warning to every shifter to keep away.

Though from the loose-hipped swagger Seth adopted before he entered the main house to check on Moira, Ethan's implied warning was merely a suggestion, not a demand.

"What I do or do not do is none of your business."

Ethan was really pissed now.

"Then you won't mind if I pursue Moira?"

The vampire wouldn't let me within a hundred yards of her heart. I knew I blew it. But Ethan didn't know.

His slight pause, followed by a wicked chuckle told me everything. "Do what you wish. Don't come crying to me if she tears your balls off."

I chuckled. "We'll see how it goes."

Ethan disconnected without another word. I smiled down at the phone.

Moira might tear my balls off, but I might have a lot of fun trying.

Considering I lived in a remote area with very little to do these days, I could use a bit of fun in my life.

CHAPTER

Seven

Seth's innate magic crackled against my skin when he walked into the kitchen. I'd lived among shifters for a while now, and while I'd never been afraid of them, I stayed wary. After everything, and the time I'd spent among Rowan's people, I realized shifters were like me, like the fae, and occasionally like the humans walking among us. Most of us were just doing our best to get by.

Things had changed for me in ways I would not have been able to comprehend a few years ago. I'd always been considered a hybrid, though I kept what I knew of my heritage mostly under wraps, but now I had one more thing living under my skin.

Living being the key word. Fee's presence lay in my heart now. Those still standing that fateful day watched her sacrifice to save Evie's mate and the other Lord, but Fee had chosen to give her last gift of magic to me—an act I still struggled with.

Why had a phoenix found me worthy? What could I possibly do to show Fee her gift was not in vain?

She wasn't quite dead. Her conscience or whatever was left in her lived inside me, The feeling was...odd. Fee didn't speak to me, but her purpose—to heal and to grant immortality—lived on inside me.

I knew I could heal. Ethan had found that out when I was on Keep property, though he assumed it was a quirk of my mixed magic. Shifters had always pegged an oddness about my scent. Whether I could grant immortality was still up in the air. If I could, I'd need to be extremely careful to keep the information to a trusted and select few.

Fee had urged me a few times, steering me toward select people, but I'd managed to resist so far.

My magic was a mixed bag. I had a deft hand with potions and charmed teas, could pull objects and fae through the realms, sort of similar to Evie's bridge powers, but with a whole lot more of a dramatic entrance, and now I could heal.

And maybe grant immortality.

Talk about a conversation starter. Yeesh.

Seth snagged a seat at the kitchen island and watched me shove snacks into the cold bag. We shouldn't be gone for too long, but you never knew. Witches were tricky even on a good day, and these sounded worse than usual.

"We gonna be gone for a week?" Seth asked, amusement simmering in his dark eyes.

"I'm expecting something to go wrong," I answered honestly. "I'd rather be safe than sorry, and you two eat like starving lions."

Seth grunted. "Don't let Soren hear you compare us to cats."

I rolled my eyes and stuffed another loaf of bread in the bag. "Is he almost done out there? We should get going soon."

Seth's lips twitched. "Should be. He had to take a phone call."

I turned to hide my grimace. I'd bet my left big toe he was on the phone with Ethan. He texted me as soon as I walked inside asking for a status update. When I told him what the real deal was with the witches, I could almost hear his fury snapping via the cell towers.

"Hope everything is okay," I said lightly.

Seth let out a hoot of laughter. "You know exactly who he's speaking to."

"I shall neither confirm nor deny."

The front door slammed open a few seconds later. Soren stomped in, stopped in the kitchen, saw me and Seth, and looked at the bag. His expression was drawn and there was a tension to the set of his jaw.

"Moira's packing for an Everest excursion," Seth said cheerfully.

Soren's brows drew together. He flicked open the bag and snorted. "Expecting trouble, Moira dear?"

"With you involved? Absolutely."

Seth laughed out loud. Soren reached over and tweaked my nose. "I have an extra heavy jacket on the hook by the back door. Grab it before we leave."

"I don't need your jacket."

Soren shrugged. "Don't take it then. Seth and I both see you trying not to shiver even when you're indoors."

I shot him an annoyed glare before turning to see the heavy down jacket right where he said it would be. Dammit. That looked extremely warm. My intolerance to the cold was becoming an issue. I was part-vampire. I should be rolling around in the snow naked laughing with glee about how the weather never affected me. Instead, I'd taken to wearing fingerless gloves and pretending I was a rich heiress who absolutely must wear cashmere all the time.

Ethan kept me in merino wool and cashmere all the time when I was there and had gone so far as to carelessly leave cardigans slung over the backs of chairs and his couches when I inevitably forgot to wear one.

I squashed thoughts of him down. Remembering how caring he was only made it hurt more when I left. I had to remember to take the man as he was, not how I wanted him to be. If he wanted to keep me in expensive warm clothing all the time, I wouldn't begrudge him. Male shifters were biologically inclined to care for the females in their lives.

While I wasn't one of his, we were linked through Evie and Rowan, and through our own experience with each other. For better or worse, Ethan chose to care for me in his own way, and I wouldn't reject those gestures just because I had a crush on him I couldn't shake.

"Thank you," I grumbled.

Soren's slight smile pissed me off, but the man had offered me a jacket, and I wasn't fool enough to say no.

Seth rose and stretched, his shirt riding up just enough to expose a sliver of well-muscled abdomen. He caught me looking and grinned.

I laughed. "Not blind, Seth. Just not interested."

"The day is still young."

Soren yanked his jacket from the hook and tossed the heavier one to me. "Let's go. The sooner we get there, the sooner we can resolve this."

"Good with me." I shrugged the jacket on.

Once we were outside, Soren took the bag of food from me and slung it over his shoulder. Seth had a smaller backpack filled with extra clothing in case of a necessary shift.

"Should we wager a little something?" I asked, staring at the stunning display of color peeking through the mountains. "If I make it there first, next time you're in Rowan's area, you'll buy me a nice dinner and a pretty pair of diamond earrings."

Soren slid me the side-eye. "You think you're going to win?"

I lifted a shoulder in a shrug. "Fifty-fifty."

Actually, the odds were much higher than that. I was fast as hell now. Genetics, training with Garrett and Ethan, and my odd magic had lent me insane speed. But these shifters didn't need to know what I could do yet.

"And if we win?" Seth asked, dark eyes glittering as he studied me.

"What do you want?"

When his grin edged toward the wicked side, I held a hand up. "Keep it strictly PG."

Seth sighed. "Every party has a pooper."

Soren studied me, a thoughtful look on his face. "A date."

All the amusement fled from my body.

"Soren," Seth warned quietly.

"You'd benefit from this, too," he growled.

Seth shook his head. "Moira, you don't have to—"

A slow, savage smile tipped my lips up. Seth and Soren both blinked. "Done, with a caveat. If I win, I want a pair of Tiffany diamond earrings, at least half a carat, in platinum, and dinner. Alone."

Seth's brows inched up toward his hairline.

Soren leaned forward, his teeth bared. "I'll make it even better. I'll get you whatever you like from Tiffany. No budget."

I blinked. Vampires, like other immortals, had to be good with money. We lived too long to squander our cash. I'd saved enough to never have to work again if I didn't want to, but I wasn't *whatever I wanted to buy at Tiffany's*. My eyes narrowed. "What's the catch?"

"If I win, we go for a weekend away."

My heart lurched. If we went away for an entire weekend, the thing might end in bloodshed. Huh. Maybe not a bad thing.

Seth cleared his throat. "Uh. What about me?"

I snorted. "You get one, too, Sethy boy."

"Hoo," Seth murmured. "Sold. Though I do not have Tiffany's money, Soren. I'll buy her dinner. You gotta take the earring debt on."

But Soren wasn't paying attention to Seth. "Do we have a deal?"

"I don't know where we're going," I said.

"Seth has a map. He'll direct you, but you'll know when we get close. You'll smell them."

That did not sound good. Was he talking about their blood or their magic?

"There's a huge oak about a hundred yards from their wards. You can't miss it. First to touch wins." Soren's eyes glimmered with the thrill of the hunt. "I ask again, do we have a deal?"

I could win. I knew I could. Seth had turned to gaze in the

direction we were going, his eyes narrowed as if he were calculating the odds, too.

"I pick the place."

Soren nodded. "No budget."

"No touching."

Soren's eyes narrowed. "Touching is allowed if you ask me."

I wouldn't. "Okay."

Seth dug the map out of his pocket.

"No shifting to wolf form," I added.

"Alright." He was staring at me so intently I felt like squirming.

Seth held the map out and pointed to a spot. I carefully examined the route, taking careful note of topography and potentially impassable points, most of which I knew wouldn't be visible on a map.

This would be a challenge. On one hand, I'd love the chance to show Soren up. On the other...spending a weekend with him would be torture. No matter what Soren said or did, we couldn't go back to where we were. Especially not after knowing some of the things he'd done.

Part of me empathized with the witches. We weren't sure he was the reason they were here, but I didn't believe in coincidences. Not like this.

I turned the wording of the deal over in my mind. Short, to the point, with concrete goals. "You got a deal."

Soren's smile made my stomach lurch. "Go."

He took off like a rocket. Seth swore and crumpled the map, shoving it into his pocket as he also took off.

I stood there like an asshole for a few seconds before letting out a growling screech and following behind.

"Cheaters!" I shouted as I took off after them.

Soren's crack of wild laughter made me snort.

CHAPTER
Eight

Vampires weren't all that common. Unlike shifters, many of us lived alone and scattered across the world, few living in close proximity to each other. Lore said we could be indiscriminate killing machines. For me, that was only true when I didn't have caffeine in the morning.

I didn't sleep in a coffin, nor did I need much blood to survive, choosing to refill maybe once every couple of months through a small vial purchased via a discreet seller. After Fee slammed into me with the force of a freight train, I hadn't needed blood since, something I was still struggling to comprehend.

Evie never asked me about how I managed my hunger. She wasn't one to pry. Everyone else assumed I had it under control, so no one knew I was on my eighth month without a refill. My stash was no longer any good, and at first, I kept repurchasing, only for each vial to go bad when another month passed without needing to refuel.

I was beginning to feel the first twinges of hunger once more, but nothing like I had before Fee. My fatigue had increased a little, though it was still minimal. If something happened and the hunger came back with a vengeance, I might have to go hunt in the woods while I waited on a shipment. But I was beginning to suspect the blood hunger was gone, and my body no longer needed it as fuel. Only time would tell.

Sometimes late at night, I wondered if I was still a vampire. Certain blood still attracted me, and I still hungered sometimes, but those instances were more craving than need. Ethan's blood sent my own pumping, and I had to stop myself from nicking him just to see what he tasted like. The Lord would never forgive me if I took something from him without permission.

My lack of need for blood hadn't dulled any of my senses. The opposite happened. Everything sharpened. My sense of smell improved so much I could smell a drop of blood from over a mile away. The first time it happened, I went to my knees with sensory overload. Only diligent practice helped my focus, and now I could tune everything out and focus on one thing.

That's what I did today. While Soren and Seth shot straight in the direction of the witches, I closed my eyes and searched for their scent. Both he and his Second had an advantage. They'd traveled there before. I was flying blind.

There. Herbal, a touch astringent, the scent of bonfire smoke woven in, and an odd touch of some kind of darker magic. And blood. So much blood.

In case they were leading me astray, I veered to the left, toward the coppery scent that told me we were not dealing with white witches. Whoever this coven was, they were using human sacrifices.

I kept Seth and Soren's scents available, ensuring I knew where they were at all times. To keep them from seeing the full extent of my abilities, I kept a slightly behind pace and stayed close enough where they could still sense me. As we ran, leaping over rocks and fallen trees, I fell into a rhythm, the crisp but warm smell of the Ponderosa pines filling my nose and lungs.

I liked this place. Wild and untouched, the forest came alive under my feet. Things hidden in burrows and holes slithered and swished, birds flew from their perches high in the trees, alarmed by our presence. The sun was slowly beginning to set, sending long purple and orange fingers over the sky.

And still we ran.

When the scent of the witches grew close, I slowly veered away from Soren and Seth, far enough where they could no longer sense my presence.

Then I opened up and let myself be me. Wind whipped my hair from its messy bun as I flew through the forest, taking insane leaps over leaf litter and rotting debris. A wild laugh broke from my throat as I ran, my arms and legs pumping in a blur. Seth and Soren were at least half a mile behind now, neither having any idea where I'd gone or what I was up to.

I pushed myself, harder and harder, the sheer joy of being able to really let myself go breaking something free in my chest. This is who I was, who I was always meant to be—something wild and uncaged, animal yet not, female yet something more. I was something to be embraced and feared, a contradiction to myself and my heritage, and something original, wholly unknown to the world. As I all but flew to my destination, that spot in my chest began to glow, so bright you could see it through my clothing and the heavy jacket I wore, Fee's purple and orange sending a glow over the trees and sky.

I touched my chest and felt the warmth. Fee, in whatever form she still existed in, was happy. Tears sprang to my eyes. "Hi, Fee," I whispered.

A pulse of bright blue answered.

I smiled and kept running, letting Fee enjoy the moment just as much as I was.

HALF AN HOUR LATER, Soren came into view, skidding to a halt gape-mouthed at my presence by the tree. Seth skidded to a stop beside him and let out a loud crack of laughter.

"Goddammit," Seth said, slapping his thighs. "I knew she was going to win!"

"She shouldn't have," Soren snarled, his eyes narrowing as he studied me.

I sat against the trunk and gave the men a little wave. "Hello, boys."

"How." A ring of gold outlined his irises.

I studied my nails. "A girl never reveals her secrets, Lord."

Seth let out a low whistle. "How much are you gonna peg him for?"

I'd been contemplating the answer while waiting. "The Tiffany Victoria Mixed Cluster Drop earrings, please."

Neither man would know the price. Seventy thousand was a good start to buying my silence.

Soren whipped out his phone and searched. A shrill hiss sounded from between his teeth. "Fucking hell, Moira."

"A deal's a deal," I said sweetly.

Seth's eyes widened as his gaze bounced between us like a tennis match. "Twenty?"

I shook my head and jerked my thumb up.

Seth blinked. "Fifty?"

I grinned and motioned upward again.

His low chuckle made Soren's jaw tighten. "Let's hope your dinner tastes are a little less high class. I'm a working man, darling."

He stuck his thumbs through his belt loops and pretended to hike his pants up.

"There's a burger place in Emberwood aptly called Ember's. I'll text you my order."

"A burger." His grin widened. "I got the better part of this deal, boss."

Soren's nostrils flared. "How'd you win?" he asked again.

All the Lords hated losing. Guess winning was ingrained into their DNA.

Telling him would only make him madder, and I liked having something to lord over him. "I already told you it was none of your business."

He turned in a slow circle, studying the lay of the land. There were no advantages out here, though he couldn't be sure I hadn't cheated because Evie hadn't ceded control over the land. It was feasible I'd come onto the land beforehand and made things easier on myself, but he would have scented me around this area and he knew it.

His jaw tightened. "Fine. Send it to the Keep?"

"Care of Evie Quinn," I added with a bright smile.

A few clicks later and I had a pair of ridiculous diamond earrings on the way to Evie's house. My bestie was going to get a kick out of this when I told her what happened.

When Soren finally dropped it, I jerked a thumb over my shoulder. "They're doing dark magic in there. Awful stuff with human sacrifices. Are you sure you want to do this?"

Soren's lips thinned. "A certain vampire told me I had to."

I'd been here for a while, and even this far away, the scent of their horrific magic was cloying to my senses. But there was something else I needed to tell him, something neither he nor Seth had picked up on yet. "That's before I smelled shifter blood inside those wards."

Soren and Seth froze.

Seth took a step forward and lifted his nose into the air, inhaling deeply. Soren watched him, and when Seth gave him a sharp shake of his head, Soren stepped up next to his Second and did the same thing.

When they both turned to me with quizzical looks, I tapped the side of my nose. "Vampires have always had keener senses. We may not be better trackers, but we scent blood like a great white. There's shifter blood behind those wards, Lord. Mark my words. Are you missing anyone?"

Seth shook his head. "Our numbers are low, but as of this morning, everyone's accounted for."

"If we drop the wards, you'll be able to scent the shifter in question. If we leave now, we can regroup and figure out a way to take them out. An apology seems dumb in hindsight, Soren. I don't think you should approach them directly."

Yes, he was an idiot for sleeping with eight witches in the same coven. The fact didn't make me want him dead, though. If he walked up to those wards, the odds were high they'd sling a spell at him before a word left his mouth.

"She's right," Seth said, seeing the wisdom in my words.

But Soren was staring toward the direction of the coven. We were still too far away to see any of the witches, but their presence weighed on my mind like an oily substance.

"There's one who will listen to reason."

I shook my head. "Bad idea. Maybe two years ago she would have, but things have changed. I can't imagine you'd sleep with someone who smelled the way that coven does now. Would you?"

He inclined his head. "I wouldn't. But I still think she will listen."

"I can't protect you without revealing myself," I said.

"Then we lure her out," Seth said.

"This is a terrible idea," I warned them.

"Then it's a good idea you're with us, so we can blame you," Soren drawled.

I gave him the bird and rose, slapping the leaves from the back of my pants and thighs. "Alright then, spill. Tell me how you're going to lure one witch out without alerting the rest."

Soren held his cell up and waved it in front of my face. "Through the magic of cellular. I'm going to text her."

Seth snorted. "Sorcery," he agreed.

"You still have her number?" If Soren had a physical little black book, it'd be a thousand pages. I wonder how much storage all the phone numbers took up inside his phone.

He didn't respond, instead typing out a quick message on his phone. "Now we wait."

To my enduring horror, the woman responded almost immediately. From the smile on Soren's face, her response was not the ass chewing I expected. "She sent me a location outside the wards and asked me to meet her there in half an hour."

Seth and I looked at each other. "Could be a trap," he said.

"How far away is she from that spot?" I asked Soren.

"Fifteen minutes give or take a few."

I chewed on the side of my lip. "Too short notice to spring anything other than a prepared spell on him."

The best spells took a lot of time and care to craft. Potions worked in a pinch, some better than others, but if they wanted Soren dead, they would have delayed him by at least a day.

"What do you think?" I asked Seth.

"I'll be there with him."

Soren glared.

"Yes, I know you can take care of yourself," Seth said with an eye roll, "but in case she has a nasty surprise up her sleeve, you should have someone there with you. I'll stay downwind. She won't know I'm around."

Witches had good senses, but they weren't up to par with a shifter or vampire.

"I'll stay close, too." Since we'd established I could move faster than either of them, I was best suited to respond quickest and get Soren out if need be.

"I'll set it up," Soren said, a grumble of disagreement in his voice.

"Send the location to us," Seth said.

A few minutes later, we all left to scope out the meetup spot. If they tried to kill Soren, doing so in the middle of nowhere was a good spot.

CHAPTER
Nine

Of course the witch was a stunner. Long auburn hair fell to her waist and swayed with every step she took. Her nose was pert and had a slight tilt at the end, reminding me of those popular filters some of the so-called influencers used when they were hocking their newest brand deal. Her eyes were wide and green, a telltale sign of a pure-blood witch.

No one knew why pure bloods had green eyes, though I heard it had something to do with the type of magic running through the firstborn witch's bloodline. Whoever this was could be powerful—probably was powerful.

She looked harmless, which instantly put me on edge. The woman was short, hitting five feet tall if she were lucky, and petite, looking like a bite-sized snack next to Soren. Something ugly twisted in my stomach. Not jealousy. Closer to self-loathing if I was being completely self-aware. I did not look like her.

Not even a little.

I was tall and pale and too thin and had eyes so dark they were almost black, with the long hair to match. I had the accessories of an Italian woman with the complexion of a Swedish milkmaid.

This witch's skin had a tinge of a golden glow to her skin and a perfectly poreless face.

Hmm. I squinted, seeking the edges of a spell or something to —Ha. A glamour.

I wanted to crow to the heavens. So she wasn't perfect. I wondered if that was her real face. Soren recognized her, so either it was, or this was a glamour she rarely removed.

The idiotic Lord allowed the woman to bring him in for an embrace.

I tensed as I searched for the flash of a knife or the telltale hint of a spell.

But the hug was just a hug, and Soren pulled away, smiling at the witch.

A tinge of pink touched the witch's cheeks. "I'm surprised you called."

Her voice was breathy and sweet, and she twisted her fingers together—a nervous gesture that didn't seem feigned.

Soren bowed his head. "I wanted to come and personally apologize."

The witch blinked. "What?"

"I know we left things…open."

Oh gods. What a moron. If I wasn't concealed high up in a tree right above them, I'd let out a groan.

"Open?" she echoed, a small furrow appearing between her brows. "You ghosted me."

Soren's jaw tightened just a hair. "And for that, I'm sorry."

Oh man. He was lying. I could smell it in the air. This SOB wasn't sorry at all. I closed my eyes for a brief second, close to feeling empathy for the witch. Maybe she *should* stab him.

I might even look the other way and let her get in a few licks.

"You're sorry," the witch said slowly, her eyes narrowing. She crossed her arms over her chest.

If I wasn't worried about Soren dying a horrible death and me getting blamed for it, I might have laughed. He was in deep shit, and I don't think he even knew it.

Even if the witch wasn't full of murderous rage, she was full of the feminine kind, and sometimes, that was just as dangerous.

Soren rubbed a hand through his hair. "Yeah, Lily. I mean, I was going through some stuff, you know?"

The way he sounded was so...

Ugh.

Had I truly fallen for this act? Soren never spoke to me like that, not with that shitty, condescending tone, but that slight wheedle in his tone sounded familiar.

I was such an idiot. My heart hardened as I listened to the bullshit pouring from his mouth. From the look on her face, Lily felt the same way.

Her foot started tapping. "Everyone is going through some *stuff*, Soren."

The witch scoffed.

As I sat there listening, I had a horrible realization. Lily had no idea Soren was involved with seven of her coven mates. There was no way she knew. She was far too calm.

No one was that good of an actress.

"Was there someone else? Did you have a girlfriend or something?"

I closed my eyes and wondered what kind of bad karma I'd racked up to get stuck in this moment.

Soren rubbed the back of his neck. "Not when we met. I was still hung up on my ex, though. And after the intense night we shared—"

I let out a silent gag.

Lily made a sympathetic click of her tongue. "Oh, Soren. I had no idea."

I rolled my eyes, grinning as I thought about what Seth was thinking from two trees over.

The witch ran her hands over Soren's chest, smoothing down the nonexistent wrinkles on his pullover. "Well, you're here now. Can't we make up for lost time?"

I swear to the gods if he pulled that witch into a bush, I'd kill him myself.

"I almost brought flowers," Soren murmured. "But I realized how foolish it was to haul them through all that terrain."

Idiot. No he didn't.

My ass was starting to hurt from the hard, rough tree bark. I pulled out my cell, hid the telltale light of the screen in my jacket, and sent a text.

Move it along. I want to get closer to the wards to see what we're dealing with.

He murmured excuses and pulled his phone out.

There's no one else around. Go and check them out while I'm here with Lily.

He definitely wanted to pull that poor witch into a bush.

Fine.

I gently eased myself into a standing position and peered overhead. The wards were quite a way ahead, but it would only take me a moment to get there.

Stay with Soren. I'm going ahead to check out their wards.

Can you believe this fucking guy? came the almost immediate response.

I grinned and tucked my phone into my jacket pocket.

A moment later, I leapt from the tree limb clear across the area, silently landing atop a tree several feet away, the slight rustle of leaves the only sound to give away my presence. Lily didn't tense or look away, caught up in Soren's intense gaze.

Shaking my head, I made one more leap before landing on the soft earth. With one more look back, I turned and headed toward the wards.

Soren was a Lord. If he couldn't handle a single witch, he shouldn't hold his title. Seth would back him up if need be, but the guy might get an eye and an earful if things progressed much farther.

Grinning at Seth's predicament, I continued walking until the soft glow of magic stopped me in my tracks.

I was still far enough away from the wards to avoid detection, but a hint of magic swirling through the air gave me pause. Stopping right at the edge of the odd glimmer, I studied the soft pink, blue, and purple shimmer, wondering if I was seeing this because of my odd magic.

I felt nothing—a complete absence of magic. Hmm. Touching the shimmer seemed like a bad idea. I sent a message to Evie.

Less than a minute later, Cernunnos, Evie's father, stood right next to me.

"Shit." I jerked away in surprise. "A little warning next time?"

He merely smiled, his ancient swirling eyes giving off a multi-colored glow as he watched me. "Jumpy, Moira?"

"Only when gods sneak up on me," I muttered.

"I am the most equipped to help you, and I must admit, you intrigue me."

I frowned. "Please don't start with the gods touched stuff again."

He'd started calling me that after the battle at Caelan's Keep when I was exposed to multiple forms of magic. The incident had changed me, giving me some uncomfortable powers I still didn't really know how to use. Unlike Evie, I wasn't actively trying to suppress my magic. Not knowing how to use the power was a deterrent, but I was slowly figuring things out.

A flash of a smile. "You still are, but you're hiding one more thing, aren't you?"

Evie had kicked him and all the other fae out after Rowan's death, but before Fee made her sacrifice. Neither one of us told him what Fee had done, but I wasn't surprised to know he either knew or suspected what lived inside me.

I debated what to say. Cernunnos and I had an odd relationship. Sometimes I thought he was flirting with me, but then I'd knock myself back down to earth. Did an ancient creature who had to work hard to pretend to be less *other* know how to flirt? Sometimes, when I caught him studying me like an interesting insect, I suspected he wanted to kill me or at least take me apart and examine my pieces. And every once in a great moon, I caught him staring at me with a little more interest than a male should have in his daughter's best friend.

Men, as a general rule, confused the hell out of me. Cernunnos was on an entirely different level. I treated him with deference because he was a god, and I was a peon, and I wasn't stupid enough to think I could ever stand against him.

Not that I'd need to. Cernunnos might be an odd duck, but I think he knew his daughter well enough to know if he came after me, Evie would never forgive him. Considering her power level now, even if he was thinking about taking me out, his daughter's wrath would give him pause.

"Why are you looking at me so?" he asked.

"I can't quite figure you out."

He tilted his head in that uncanny valley way he had about him. Cernunnos was the type of male who never, no matter how much he tried, would appear human.

To be fair, he didn't try all that hard. For Evie's sake, he did, and he'd relaxed a little about some things. Like tonight, for example, he wore his ever-popular choice of joggers and a long-sleeved t-shirt, and tennis shoes with no-show socks. Very Gen-X and elder millennial.

His hair was a shaggy mess around his head. No mossy antlers or buckskin in sight.

"Do you need to figure me out?" he asked.

"Suppose not," I said with a grunt.

His gaze lingered on my profile. "You're concerned about this magic, I take it?"

Cernunnos lifted his hand, less than a quarter of an inch from the magic, a slight furrow on his handsome face. "Evangeline said this was of witch make?"

I nodded. "Odd, isn't it?"

"Indeed."

Like me, Cernunnos chose not to touch the strange magic.

Instead, he walked along the border, his fingers tracing just above the surface. I followed behind him on silent feet, watching to see what he would do.

"The ward they want you to believe is the main one is farther out," he mused. "This is the true one." He glanced back at me. "You shouldn't be able to see this, little vampire."

Bully for me. I gave him an awkward smile. Too late to deny it. Evie already told on me.

"What happens if we touch it?" I asked.

Cernunnos grinned. "Want to find out?"

Huh. It'd been a while since I had some fun. With the god by my side, we could do a lot of damage without worrying about getting overwhelmed.

But alas, I was here to find out why they were here. Not to fuck up their day.

Maybe I could do both.

I explained what Soren had done, and watched with delight as Cernunnos's eyebrows inched up, so high on his face, his forehead looked like an artist's depiction of a sound wave. "Eight?"

His tone sounded so disbelieving it made me laugh. "Eight. In one coven."

He shook his head. "Idiot. Any male worth his salt should know if a woman is worthy, he won't have the time or the inclination for another."

I blinked. Aww. That was surprisingly sweet. "I think this is a number's game more than anything. Soren has deep-seated issues."

Cernunnos rolled his eyes. "Your young Lord is addicted to attention, Moira, and terribly vain to boot. His only issue is his ego."

"I think it's more complicated than that," I said quietly. "Soren isn't one to talk about his past, but I've always wondered if there was someone he loved and lost."

The god shook his head. "If that is true, he should thank the gods for the gift he was given and hold those memories close, not sully them with every pretty thing that comes along. Physical beauty is fleeting in a human, my dear. Most witches are not immortal. Soren seeks those he knows he will never mate with—playthings he can enjoy and discard after a little while."

I stared at Cernunnos for a long moment, some hard-won realizations slamming into me like a truck.

"Ah," he said softly. "He tried with you."

I looked away.

"He did not succeed," Cernunnos said with certainty. "You would carry his smell."

First of all, eww. Second, I hated that every paranormal could tell our business based on our smell. Maybe when the tea shop really got going and I made all the money I invested back, I'd open an apothecary and come up with a potion to hide shit like that. Who I slept with was none of anyone's business but my own.

I closed my eyes and exhaled. "He did not," I confirmed. "Things are complicated between us."

A warm hand touched my arm. Cernunnos gently turned me to face him. He lifted his hand and cupped my cheek. "Soren is a fool," he murmured. "I do not say this to hurt you, but I believe he genuinely cares for you and does not know how to do anything other than what he's always done. If you looked, I am certain you would see the Lord never messes with other immortals. His conquests have always been humans or witches or those who are not long-lived. I know it may not feel like it now, but you are special to him. He just went about it in a terrible way."

He was right. Knowing that didn't make me feel any better. In fact, it made me feel worse because I suspected Cernunnos was right. I'd never smelled an immortal on Soren, other than the scents of his Pack or the other Lords when their meetings went long. However, he carried the faint scents of human women and witches, something I never put together until this moment.

Cernunnos dropped his hand. "You deserve better than a man too scared to show you who he is. Fight for more, little vampire."

We stared at each other, an unreadable expression lingering on his face. Man. Sometimes Evie's dad was intense as hell.

"You don't like him."

Cernunnos snorted. "Soren is an escape artist. He never makes a stand and sides with the winning party when all hope is lost. The Lord has a gift for saying flattering and ego-stroking things to the right people, and his pretty face helps him along, but there will come a time when Soren has to face what he's become." His voice dropped low. "And trust me when I say you do not want to be by his side when that day arrives."

I swallowed hard. "Soren and I will never be anything. I decided the day—"

Cernunnos didn't press. "He will not love you like you deserve to be loved. Mark my words." He turned and studied the ward once more.

"Would you like to figure out what's going on?"

"I would, but I'd rather keep my identity and scent a secret if possible."

Cernunnos smiled and waved his hand. I touched my suddenly curly hair and looked down to see a pair of unfamiliar boots and wool leggings. "They'll never know you were here."

"You're handy to have around."

The god chuckled. "Now, I cannot interfere." He rolled his eyes. "Evie's rules."

I snorted.

"But this is fae land, and the witches are unwelcome here. I have every right to tear down their wards and investigate what they're doing."

"You're like a deputy."

His face lit up. "Ah. Yes! Evie should have given me a badge."

"Bummer. It's never as cool to make your own."

He frowned. "True. Maybe I will ask her later."

This guy. I found it difficult to dislike him.

He lifted his hand and pressed his palm to the ward. His eyes flared with power for a brief moment before the magic collapsed, shattering like glass around us.

Cernunnos held out his hand. "Come, little vampire. Let's look into the witch's cauldron."

CHAPTER

Ten

Hanging out with a god was kind of cool. Especially when said god basically kicked down the doors like he was part of a paranormal swat team. The second ward fell in seconds, a wash of rot permeating through the air as soon as we stepped over the line.

"Oh," I breathed, immediately regretting it when the scent of human remains blasted me in the face. My involuntary gag made Cernunnos chuckle.

"The cycle of life is not always pretty," he mused.

A dozen witches came at us. Not all of them would have felt the first ward fall. The magic was so unique, Cernunnos suspected they had outside help. But all of them felt the second one.

Spells flew at us, but Cernunnos froze them with a swipe of his hand.

The witches stumbled, slack-jawed at his casual display of power.

"Who leads this coven?" he demanded.

A dark-haired witch stepped out from behind the others. She inclined her head at Cernunnos, surprise lingering in her green eyes. The witch looked at me for longer, her eyes narrowing.

Magic glowed in her eyes, fading after a moment. She was trying to pierce Cernunnos's glamour to no effect. Ballsy.

"I am," she said, her voice husky and feminine. Like most witches, she was beautiful, and an image of her writhing above Soren sprang into my mind unbidden.

Gods. This was stupid. I didn't even like him all that much, but my ego was bruised, and I couldn't stop thinking about eight of these damn witches. Was one of them her?

The witch's lips curved in a smile. "To what do I owe the pleasure, Horned God? I apologize we have not made appropriate deference to you. We were unaware you walked these lands."

Ooh. Flattery will get you nowhere. Not with Cernunnos anyhow. "I do not take human sacrifices, witchling."

From the almost undetectable flinch, Cernunnos's use of the term describing an inexperienced, young witch stung. Her lips tightened.

"From the smell, you've sacrificed many innocent lives for your spell work. What is it you are trying to accomplish?"

The witch looked at me one more time.

"Do not worry about my companion," he chided. "She is with me by my choice and my choices do not concern you."

The rebuke made her jaw tighten. "We are merely practicing for the promotion of one of our sisters. She is about to take the position of High Priestess in our sister coven."

Liar. I smelled it all over her. The witch was good at controlling her emotions, but I was a vampire and Cernunnos was a god. Her fingers, trapped inside her voluminous robes, held a fine tremor, and her heartbeat had sped up.

"Are you registered as a dark magic coven?" Cernunnos asked mildly.

Holy shit. Was that even a thing? I did my best to keep the surprise off my face. Maybe Cernunnos and I should team up and form a paranormal detective agency where we tear down wards and bust bad guys. We could call it Vamp Gods ™ and charge outrageous rates for our services.

At the end of every case, we'd go have a beer and bust each other's chops for our poor dating choices, then do it all again the next week. What a life that would be.

"We are a relatively new coven and—"

"Your lies are wasted on us. I will ask you again. Are you registered as a dark magic coven?"

The witch swallowed, her eyes darting nervously from me to Cernunnos.

"No, your majesty."

Oooh. She busted out the majesty. Girlfriend knew she was in deep shit now.

"Why not?" His voice was mild, almost uninterested, but antlers were slowly growing from his head, and his clothing was morphing from that of a young athletic coach to the god of legend.

A fine bead of sweat had broken out on the witch's forehead. Her coven members were frozen with fear, their eyes wide and still on Cernunnos. When he spoke again, his voice morphed into a thing of fearsome beauty—a savage and wild sound, the rumble like an unexpected thunderstorm.

"Tell me what business you have on fae lands."

The witch pulled her hands from her robe and wrung them nervously. "We are searching for someone, Your Majesty. Someone who wronged us."

"Not just searching," Cernunnos said. "You could have easily done that in one's living room with a single piece of hair or cloth-ing. Elaborate."

Another witch stepped up. The leader's lips thinned. "You are not needed, Elladora. Return to your place."

Cernunnos held a hand up. "Do you wish to speak, young witchling?"

She whispered something to their leader who shook her head sharply.

"Speak!" Cernunnos commanded.

The younger witch had hazel eyes—not pureblooded, but her

eyes were dominant green, so at least half. She was pretty in a girl next door way, not the poreless, shining beauty of the others with bright green eyes. With them standing so close together, I suspected their leader was immortal. The younger witch might be long-lived, but she had a very human air about her.

Something about her put me slightly at ease. "Someone has wronged us, Your Majesty."

My stomach sank. Fucking Soren.

"We are here to right the wrong."

"Do you know whose property you trespass on?"

She shook her head. "No, I am sorry. We can move."

Cernunnos studied her. "You will need to move several states, child. This land belongs to the fae queen."

Everyone's eyes widened at that one. Evie wasn't one to plant a flag and scream about her victory. This land used to be controlled by Donovan, one of the Shifter Lords who met an untimely end. When a Lord died, no one advertised the news. Another Lord was quietly chosen and moved onto the territory for them to stake their claim both on the land and through its people.

Evie took the land from Donovan and refused to allow another Lord to live on the property. She'd done Soren a great favor by allowing him to bring some of his Packmates to reside here—a decision I was sure she was regretting right about now.

From the looks on their faces, none of them knew about Evie's claim to the land. Cernunnos was technically within his rights to kill them all where they stood.

And they knew it. The other witches began whispering among themselves, a few looking to the darkness of the woods beyond.

"I wouldn't try it," I said. "We'll catch you within seconds."

The leader spun around and hissed a warning at the others before turning back around. "We will leave. Immediately."

"Tell me about this person who wronged you," Cernunnos demanded.

She licked her lips. "He is a man of no importance to you, Your

Majesty. His crimes are for us to answer, not someone of such high standing as yourself."

Dear gods. This witch knew how to lay it on thick.

"I will be the judge of this man's importance."

Annoyance at her defeat flickered in her eyes. "He has lain with most of our coven."

The younger witch stiffened.

"And one of them is with child."

The floor bottomed out from my feet. I swayed where I stood. That was impossible.

Unless...

"How long ago?" I croaked. Tears burned the back of my eyes, and I squashed the betrayal down.

The witch looked at me. "Six months."

Truth.

Soren had lied right to my face, and I hadn't smelled the untruth on him. He said he'd been with them two years ago and implied he hadn't been with anyone since me.

"Bring the witch," Cernunnos said, defeat in his voice. He edged slightly closer to me, his body heat warming the cold edges of my soul.

A stunning witch with wide green eyes stepped forward. Cernunnos stepped up to her and placed his hand on her abdomen. His eyes flared with power for a brief second.

"Who is the father?" Cernunnos asked.

She licked her lips and glanced at her leader. The witch nodded.

"Lord Soren."

I closed my eyes for a split second, but an odd scent hit me.

Lie.

The witch was lying. My eyes flew open. Cernunnos slowly shook his head and came back to my side.

"Your witch is not pregnant with a shifter's child," he said gently. "Regardless of Lord Soren's otherwise appalling behavior, he has not begotten a child on anyone here."

The lead witch's eyes widened. Her attention snapped to the young witch who bowed her head and sobbed.

"I'm sorry!" She turned and ran, not getting far before the other witches grabbed her.

"What will happen to her?" I asked.

"We would never harm a witch's unborn child," she said. "Her punishment will occur once the child is born, and it is not for you to get involved. Witch business is private within covens."

"You will vacate this place by six a.m.," Cernunnos said. "If you do not, I will come back and raze your coven to the ground."

The witch opened her mouth, thought better about it, then closed her mouth. "Very well, Your Majesty."

"I do not interfere in mortal meddlings," he said. "Nor do I hold dominion over witches. Take your revenge if you must—"

My head snapped his direction. Godsdammit, Cernunnos. He could have told them to drop all their nonsense against Soren and they probably would have. Then I could have gone home!

"But know if you strike the Lords, they will strike back twice as hard. Be prepared, witchlings."

She dipped her head in acknowledgment. "Noted, Your Majesty."

A tense silence occurred. Cernunnos wasn't done. "What strange magic created your outer ward?"

The other witches started murmuring again. They were really bad about keeping things chill. If they pretended not to know, Cernunnos might not punish all of them, depending on the answer.

A familiar scent began to leak around us, overshadowing even the rank smell of human remains. I froze in place, my heartbeat hammering against my ribs. Sweat pooled at the small of my back, and fear iced through my veins.

I knew that smell.

Cernunnos stepped closer and gave me an odd look.

"The magic is mine, Your Majesty." The voice belonged to no one.

But I knew the sound.

A woman appeared from thin air. Tall, stunning, and the evilest person I'd ever met in my entire life stood before us.

I stifled the whimper threatening at the back of my throat and kept my expression currently blank. Inside, I was screaming, horror and pain and raw, unfettered terror flooding through my veins.

Cernunnos knew something was wrong but stood his ground. He inclined his head. "And you are?"

A delicate and pale hand capable of unfathomable cruelty touched her ample chest. "My apologies. My name is Minka Belyaev."

That was not her name.

I should know.

The woman standing before me had given birth to me in an alley several hundred years ago.

CHAPTER
Eleven

I was drowning on dry land. No idea how long Cernunnos stood talking to the woman calling herself Minka; no clue what they spoke about. The only thing I knew was fear and horror, and if the earth would have swallowed me up in that moment, I would have gone gladly.

Evie knew nothing about my former life, only a mix of truths and untruths, the lies much bigger than the small glimpses I'd allowed her.

I told her I didn't know my father. True. I think I told her I was placed into another home at thirteen. Also true, but I didn't correct her when Evie once assumed I'd spent my entire life in foster care.

I told her I was ninety-something. Lie.

I could no longer remember the truths or the lies I'd told, and because of it, I avoided speaking of my past. Not because I was ashamed, but because I wouldn't be able to bear the look in Evie's eyes when she knew the horrors I'd undergone.

White noise roared between my ears, turning everything muffled and static. Phantom pain began in my feet and pricked up my calves to my knees and thighs, the remembrance of a hot poker digging into my skin followed by the subsequent scarring and limping. The realization she could have something more permanent to brutalize led her to search the land for a vampire without the scruples to care that turning a child was breaking all the cardinal rules of their kind.

I was aware enough to know this woman did not know who I was. Cernunnos's glamour held even against her disturbing stare, and I shoved my hands in my pockets so no one would see how they shook.

My mouth was dry, each breath a painful drag of air. I needed to go. I needed to get away from this smell, from this place, from these witches, from her—oh gods, I was dying and everything hurt and how could this be happening to me—

Wind tore at my skin and hair, a frigid blast of cold ripping through the world.

"*Breathe*, Moira," a savage voice commanded.

"I—I—I can—can't—" My teeth chattered. "Sh—sh—sh—"

Strong warm arms wrapped around me, someone tugging me into the curve of their body. Blessed heat I wanted to burrow inside. "Moira. One breath, *cridhe daor*. Just one."

A warm hand on my back rubbed circles. I dragged in a breath, only to let out a harsh, racking sob.

"There," the voice murmured. "Another."

When the sobs finally came, I couldn't stop them. I was helpless as a babe outside in a thunderstorm. Hot, furious tears streamed from my eyes, and I was embarrassed and tried to stop but couldn't, and so they came and came and came, and the male I was wrapped around didn't tell me to stop or chastise me.

He simply held me until I was a burned-out shell, too exhausted to do anything but blink up at the ceiling.

Cernunnos held me, a warm hand toying with the strands of my hair. I stiffened and tried to extricate myself, but his arms tightened.

"No."

A simple command and one I thought I should resist but was too tired to try.

We sat in a cozy room with wood paneled walls and glossy wood flooring. A fireplace burned merrily a few feet away, the soft pop and crackle of wood the only sound besides our breathing. The furnishings were sparse and well loved. A couch with a burnished-wood frame was opposite us, next to a well-used navy-blue recliner.

The coffee table was scarred and nicked but well cared for, a handful of books scattered across the surface. A colorful rug lay underneath, mixed with gorgeous shades of blue, maroon, and cream.

There was a kitchen close by, a small area with a stove, a retro-looking fridge, and a sink. No microwave or any modern appliances. A dented percolator sat on top of the stove.

"Where am I?"

"My home. It is not much, but I can have anything I want and choose to live simply. The world has too much noise, and I like to come here when I want to be quiet."

"It's lovely," I murmured, knowing he would sense the truth in my words.

A pause, followed by a surprised tone. "Truly?"

I nodded, my head against his lean chest. "It suits you."

His hand hadn't stopped rubbing circles over my back. "Would you like to talk about it?"

"Would you tell Evie?"

A tear slipped down my nose.

"She doesn't know?"

"No one knows."

He inhaled a heavy breath. "Moira."

My fists clutched his shirt. "Cernunnos. No. You cannot tell her about this. Please."

"I will not agree to lie to my daughter."

I stiffened and was about to extricate my way out even if I had to fight until he said the next words.

"If Evie does not ask, then I will not tell her. I will never bring up your pain, Moira. Never. You have my word."

My eyes closed. "Thank you," I whispered.

"I hid your pain from that woman as soon as I sensed it. I assumed you would have revealed yourself to her if you wanted her to know your identity." His voice turned gentle. "You know her."

No. I'd never known her. I'd only known her cruelty. "She's my mother."

A sharp inhalation. "She was…not good to you."

I shook my head.

"Ah," he breathed. "I've known no greater pain in my life than being without my daughter. Being intentionally cruel to someone you created is the most egregious of sins."

"Tell me what she said."

The circles paused. "Moira. You can change the subject with Evie and dodge her questions, but I pulled you out of your own personal hell. While I do not demand an explanation, I would like one. Your phone has been ringing off the hook. Ethan is beside himself—"

I stiffened. "How does Ethan know what happened?"

"You will have to ask him yourself, little vampire."

I frowned.

"Soren had to retreat after the witches decided since I gave them the timeline of vacating by tomorrow, they should make their move tonight."

Well shit. "Is he alright?"

"While I believe dying would teach the Lord a valuable, albeit permanent, lesson, I thought you might be upset if I allowed him to perish while on your watch. I sent aid."

He sounded amused.

I popped my head up and peered at him. "What kind of aid?"

"A team of cat shifters owed me a favor." His chest rumbled with a chuckle. "Soren was involved with one of their members not too long ago. Should be an entertaining time."

My lips twitched. "Serves him right for being a total hoe."

"Indeed. Now, Moira. Tell me why you flared with magic and began to glow when fear paralyzed you."

I dipped my head, but Cernunnos lifted my chin with his index finger. "And tell me why, when you dropped all your guards, I smelled dark magic surfacing deep within your blood."

Twelve

ETHAN

Moira had disappeared off the face of the earth. Ignoring *why* I could feel her for the moment because that was a whole different can of worms I would never be ready to face, I focused on the *where*.

She still lived. I knew that for sure. But she was no longer in this world.

I stared at my cell for a long moment before uttering a curse. Evie would worry if I texted her, but she might know something Moira wouldn't have told me.

I fired off a quick message to the fae queen and waited.

Evie and I had an odd relationship. We started out antagonistic toward each other, most of that my fault. Now we had an uneasy truce, mostly because of Rowan.

Despite myself, I liked the young Lord, and I liked how he stood up for what was right in his quiet way. And I liked him and Evie together.

To her credit, she texted back almost right away.

I sent my father to her. He might have taken her through the bridge.

I stared at my phone. That godsdamned bridge was fast becoming the bane of our existence. It had always existed; we just didn't know its purpose until recently. With the incident at

Rowan's Keep several months ago where a fucking fae had *killed* me, I wasn't feeling too kindly toward the fae these days.

To know Moira was alone, somewhere in the fae realms with the most powerful fae in existence…I scratched under my collar. When that didn't help, I ripped off my tie and tossed it onto my desk.

"Fuck!"

ETA? I texted back.

Unknown.

Those three little dots went on for long enough to make me nervous.

She's safe with him. If he took her through the bridge, something must have gone wrong. As soon as I hear from her, I will let you know.

I let out a heavy breath.

Thank you.

Evie didn't respond again.

I tried texting Moira again, but the message came back as undelivered.

Feeling helpless was awful. I was never helpless. Ethan Flint was always prepared. There was never a situation he couldn't fix.

"And yet here you are speaking about yourself in the third person," I muttered to the air.

I tried Soren again. He picked up on the third ring.

"She's with Cernunnos. That's all I know," Soren said. "I'm a little busy here, if you don't mind."

"What happened?"

"Cats," Soren snarled. "Cats everywhere. Evie's father is a dick."

I'd had few dealings with the god. He never visited me like he did Caelan and eventually Rowan. I thought it perhaps because he could not use me for anything to further his own agenda. Gods were always bored and fickle, a lesson I learned long ago.

They find your weak points and press them so you will dance for them like a puppet.

"Can you tell me anything else?"

Soren sighed and rattled off what happened before cursing and hanging up.

She'd left Soren with the witches and gone off on her own to check out the wards. He didn't know anything other than that. Evie must have told him where she was.

Soren could handle the cats. My lips twitched. Cernunnos must know about the Lord's witch harem and disapproved.

I tossed my phone on the desk and ran my hands through my hair. This would be so much easier if she still lived here—if I could feel her on my property and know where she was at any given moment.

I'd fucked things up so horribly. And yet, I couldn't fix it. To do so would tear a piece of my soul away.

Any feelings I had for Moira had to stay locked up tight. I could care for her, take care of her, even touch her sometimes if I took care when I did so.

But I could never love her.

Not the way she deserved.

My heart belonged to someone else and always would.

CHAPTER
Thirteen

I told Cernunnos the worst of me, the secrets I long held in a dark locked box pushed deep down in my heart. And he listened, never judging, never asking questions. He merely held me and let me talk.

When I finally finished, my throat was hoarse and my soul wrung dry.

His fingers still toyed in my hair, the motion sending waves of relaxation over me. My eyes grew heavy, the fire's warmth and his body heat combining to lull me into rest.

I barely recognized Cernunnos lifting me, so tired I couldn't murmur a protest. He laid me down in a soft bed and pulled the covers over my body.

"Rest, Moira," he said quietly, his finger tracing down my jaw. "You are safe."

For once in my life, in the home of a god, I believed him.

I was safe.

Finally.

THE SMELL of woodsmoke and coffee woke me the next morning. Or I thought it was morning. Hard to tell in this realm. A hot cup of tea sat on the old nightstand. I smiled when I lifted the mug to my nose, the scent of bergamot curling through the air.

Earl Grey. Mmm. A small silver tray of cream and sugar sat beside the lamp. I doctored my tea, took a few fortifying sips of caffeine and got out of bed, my bare feet hitting warm wooden flooring. I liked this place.

It was wild, like Cernunnos, but cozy, like Evie. A glance down made me pause. The world went a little sideways when I realized I was in silk pajamas, a pale pink camisole and matching bottoms. I took a beat to remember Cernunnos did not have to undress me. The dude was made of literal magic. A small snap of his fingers and he could turn this place into a mansion and have me dripping in diamonds.

A slow breath released from my tight chest. He'd thoughtfully left a pair of slippers at the edge of the bed. I slipped them on, added the matching robe he'd slung over a chair, and walked out of the bedroom.

I felt freer today, more unburdened than I had in years. No doubt I had an issue on my hands when I returned home, but right now, I was safe in this strange cabin with a god who'd protected me at my most vulnerable.

Making a beeline for the kettle, I spotted Cernunnos sitting on the small deck, one ankle crossed over his knee. He wore a pair of cotton pants and a quarter zip pullover today, a pair of beat up boat shoes on his feet.

A chuckle slipped from my lips. He looked like a nepo baby on a mountain vacation. Once I had my mug topped off, I slid open the screen door and took the seat beside him.

This view was incredible. In the distance, mountains scraped the sky, a low fog cutting off the tips, lending a humid touch to the air. Green pine trees were everywhere, the scent of them sharp to my senses.

"Morning," he murmured.

I curled up in my seat and watched the horizon. "Morning."

"How'd you sleep?"

I thought about it and realized I didn't remember a single thing once my head hit the pillow. Unusual for me. "Better than I have in years," I admitted.

Cernunnos grunted. "You were safe. That's why."

I shrugged. "Listen, I should—"

"Do not insult me by thanking me, Moira." He sent me a disapproving look.

I blinked.

"You are my daughter's best friend, but more importantly, I feel like you are beginning to be my friend."

My heart warmed.

"Isn't that what friends do?"

I had to chuckle. "Not new friends," I admitted. "If I'd done that to someone I didn't know that well, they might have left me to fend for myself."

"Then they are not meant to be your friend."

He made it sound so simple. Maybe it was to someone like him.

"Do you have friends?" I asked.

Cernunnos shrugged, a human gesture on a male who was anything but. "It's impossible for someone like me to have true friends. I have people I can trust for small things, but who will do those things while calculating how they might be able to use the favor against me in the future."

I let out a soft gasp. "That's horrible."

He nodded, his face unreadable. "Then you understand how I wish to receive no thanks from you."

I did. "I'd never do that to you," I said quietly. "We are very different in power levels, and I'm not sure what kind of favor you'd ever need from me, but if you needed one, I would never hold it against you."

He turned to look at me, his swirling eyes ancient and terrible. "Do you swear?"

Magic lifted in the air, twirling my loose hair around my shoulders. I smiled sadly at him. "You don't need to use magic to know my vow is true, Cernunnos. It hurts my feelings you think you must." I touched my chest. "But yes, I swear it. If you ever have need of me, you can call on me no matter where I am or who I am with, and I will help you."

He stared at me for a long moment. "And you can do the same."

I felt the truth of his words in my chest. "I would never take advantage of you."

A small smile. "I know, little goddess."

His magic fell away, leaving only the fresh air and a gentle breeze. "Thank you for the tea. It's my favorite kind."

"I know. Evie told me."

I stiffened. "She knows I'm here."

"My daughter believes you were injured, and I took you to a healer in the fae realm. As far as she knows, you're staying overnight for observation. She's informed Soren and Ethan."

I sighed. "I hate that you had to lie to her."

"I didn't," Cernunnos said simply. "I chose to. This was a simple white lie, Moira, and one I will not do again. I encourage you to tell her what you told me."

My fingers tightened around my cup. "I can't."

He looked away. "Do you think after all Evie did for everyone else, she would judge you for something that was never your fault?"

"No. Never."

He fell silent for a moment. "Then I do not understand why you haven't told her about your past and the evils that have befallen you."

I wouldn't have admitted this to anyone else, and I wasn't sure why I admitted it to him, but he and I were full of firsts these days. "Because I am ashamed."

Cernunnos's eyes widened with surprise. He set his mug down and stood, turning to loom over me. He held out his hand. "Come."

I frowned. "This chair is comfy, and I haven't had a second cup of tea yet…"

He rolled his eyes and plucked me out of the chair with ease, curling my body against his chest.

"Cernunnos!"

He grinned and leapt over the edge of his deck, carrying me through the woods at a breakneck pace.

I don't know how long he ran. Just when I was starting to feel guilty for being a lazy sack of potatoes, he stopped and set me down. We stood in a fairy circle, dotted with Amanita Muscaria mushrooms, their pretty red and white caps glimmering with dew.

Note to self, gather some of those and take them home. Maybe I could convince Evie to do fae shrooms with me. She was on board for a lot more than normal shenanigans these days.

Power permeated this place, deep and ancient fae magic similar to the male I stood with.

He lifted his hand. "Come," he commanded.

Animals of all shapes and sizes thundered through the forest, stopping a respectful distance away. My breath caught in my throat. Most animals didn't mind me, but some got a little skittish. None of these animals seemed to mind my presence. In fact, they came closer once Cernunnos gestured and watched me.

An adorable red and white fox sniffed at my feet, chittered, then sat on its haunches, and stared at me. Cernunnos pressed something into my hand.

I opened my palm to see a handful of berries.

"Go ahead," he urged. "He's the most curious about you."

I slowly crouched and held open my palm. The fox watched me for a moment before slowly creeping forward, its paws silent on the moist leaf litter. It sniffed my hand before gently taking a berry and skittering a few feet away.

I smiled. "It's adorable."

"He," Cernunnos corrected. "Ember is curious to his own detriment sometimes, but he's a loyal and brave companion."

"You know all these animals by name?"

His eyes glimmered with amusement. "I know all the wild things by their name, Moira. Evie might be the fae queen, but I still rule over all animal kind."

I didn't know that. Made sense now that I was standing here surrounded by dozens of animals. "Does Evie know?"

He grinned. "If it were up to Evie, I'd be king of everything so she could grow her flowers and roll around with that husband of hers in peace."

I snorted. "True."

The fox came back and sniffed. I opened my palm to give him another berry. This time, he bumped my knee with his head and rubbed his cheek against me.

"Awww."

"Ember is asking for a head scratch."

Hesitant, I lifted my fingers. The fox rubbed his soft head against my palm. Tears sprang to my eyes. "Hi, little guy."

Cernunnos sat cross-legged on the ground. A few animals came and curled up beside him. One, a small coyote, curled up in his lap.

This was so freaking cool. I could stay out here all day. No—all year. Maybe even for the rest of my life.

"Shame is a fickle thing, Moira."

My body went stiff.

"The emotion is triggered by outer occurrences and our inner self. Everything you went through was chosen to degrade you. Nothing that happened to you was your fault. You were an innocent, tender child forced to grow up far too soon. The only shame in that is the loss of your childhood."

"I know all of this," I said, my voice hoarse despite the early hour.

"Your mind knows," he said gently. "Your body still holds on tight, clinging to what it knows."

I sank to the ground. Ember sniffed at my knee, looked up at me, and put one paw on my thigh.

I patted my lap, not thinking for a moment that he'd curl up with me, but the fox surprised me. In one pounce, Ember was in my lap, curled into a little apostrophe, his tail tucked around his head. My hand rested on his side, gently running my fingers through his fur.

Somehow, Ember knew I needed comfort. Animals were far smarter than humans gave them credit for.

"How do I fix this?" I asked.

Cernunnos said nothing for a little while. "How are you feeling today?"

I frowned. "Better than yesterday."

"Better than before yesterday?"

I knew what he was getting at. "It helped to talk about it," I grumbled.

"Humans and paranormals are more alike than they think. You, gods touched, are less like them and more like us, but your heart remains firmly human. Evie loves you more than anyone in her life, maybe even more than her Rowan. If there is anyone who will understand, it's her."

"I've lied to her for years."

"Evie lied to everyone, too. She will not judge you for protecting yourself when she did the same thing to everyone else in her life."

He was right. "I'll try."

"Good." He reached out for the deer snuffling his shoulder and patted it on the nose. "We have to go back soon."

"I know."

"Where would you like to go?"

"Home, if you don't mind." I glanced down at myself. "Can I keep the pajamas?"

"Of course." He paused. "You like them?"

"I'd be a fool not to appreciate real silk in pajama form."

He offered a small smile. "Good. I was not sure what to do last night. Sleeping in boots and a jacket seemed uncomfortable."

I reached over and patted his arm. "Thank you."

Cernunnos inclined his head. "You are welcome, Moira."

We sat in silence until the sun was high overhead. Even then, the temperature remained cool. "Should we go back?"

I sighed. "We should. My cell doesn't work here. I probably have a dozen messages and missed calls."

He glanced at me. "It most certainly does. I hope you don't mind, but I silenced those calls. There have been no emergencies."

On one hand, that was a little presumptive. On the other, this was the most quiet I'd had in years. "Alright, but next time, please ask."

"Deal."

I looked down at Ember. "Aww. He's so peaceful I hate to move him."

"Would you like to take him with you?"

I gawked at Cernunnos. "What? This is his home?"

"Rowan has hundreds of acres, does he not?"

"Err. Yes. But it's full of wolves and bears! Would he get eaten?"

He laughed. "No. Ember is a being of magic. He also happens to be a clever fox."

I stroked a hand down Ember's soft fur. "I don't want to take him away from this place. It's amazing."

"Very well." He smiled down at the sleeping fox. "But do not be surprised if Ember finds you of his own volition when he realizes you are gone."

With that, I carefully eased the fox from my lap into a soft pile of leaves and took Cernunnos's hand.

I could no longer put off the inevitable.

"I know you're there," I said to the darkness as I tossed my keys onto the kitchen counter and kicked off my shoes.

My living room lamp flicked on, revealing Ethan in the shadows. He hadn't shaved in at least a day, giving him a rugged, dangerous look. His eyes looked black in the low light, the irises outlined with a soft ring of gold.

I paused. "Ethan?"

"Where have you been?"

His emotions were running high, but I was not his wife or his girlfriend. "You broke into my home. Again. We talked about this, Ethan. This is my space, and you need permission to enter."

He ignored everything I said. "Where have you been?"

I shrugged my jacket off and filled the kettle with water. "You know where I've been."

"You smell like him," he growled.

That one wasn't worth a response. I brought two mugs down from the cabinet. Few people liked tea as much as I did, but Ethan would drink whatever I put in front of him with no complaint. Setting a tea strainer filled with a teaspoon of Earl Grey in each mug, I set them aside to wait for the water to finish boiling.

"Did you hear me?"

I ignored him again, the tension in the air scratching at the back of my neck. The kettle finally signaled. I filled both mugs, added a little cream and stirred.

When I looked at Ethan once more, there was no midnight left in his eyes. The gold was so warm and bright, it cast a molten glow over my living room.

I clicked my tongue and pushed a mug at him. "Drink," I demanded.

The command made him frown, but Ethan took the mug, the gesture stiff. He didn't want to listen to me, but I was taking care of him and no male shifter would ignore his urge.

I curled into my reading chair and sipped my tea, waiting for Ethan to calm the hell down.

Our time together blurred boundaries. There was an undeniable physical element to our relationship—casual touches and brushes of hands over skin—but never any heated intimacy. Ethan wouldn't allow such, and I respected his needs.

Only later had I realized in doing so, I'd ignored my own.

He lifted the mug and sipped. I waited a full five minutes for that glow in his eyes to die.

"You are not my mate," I said matter-of-factly. "You are not my husband, my boyfriend, or my lover. I have the right to come home smelling like any male or female I wish. I can take a lover—fae, shifter, Lord, human, vampire…whatever I wish, and you have no right to question me about my decision."

That glow started up again. He opened his mouth to argue. I lifted my hand. "I'm not finished, Ethan."

"We've had this conversation before. I can't continue doing this. You've made your wishes clear multiple times. You've said you don't want me. This time I'm choosing to believe you. If you don't want me, stop breaking into my home and demanding explanations you don't deserve."

"Moira." He was hanging on the edge of violence. "You can't—"

"I can, and I will. When I lived at your Keep, you are the one who pushed our intimacy into something other than just friends. Even then I respected your rules." I slowly shook my head. "But I don't deserve this hot and cold treatment you're giving me. I deserve to be held and loved and taken care of, and I deserve a man who does all of those things—not just one and demands me to behave as if he's all three."

Ethan's nostrils flared. "You don't understand."

"You're right. I don't. And you've never helped me understand your reasoning. I—" This is where things could all go wrong. I had to tread lightly.

"There must have been someone in your life you loved so much."

He went rigid, his knuckles turning white around the mug.

"We all deserve to have that in our life at least once," I said softly. "You trying to prevent me from having such is unfair and you know it."

Ethan's eyes took on the strange tinge of gold and blue. "I can't."

I dipped my head. "I know."

Moisture glimmered in his eyes. "Whoever she was to make you love her so fiercely must have been wonderful, Ethan. I'm so glad you had someone who loved you like you deserved."

He looked away, then down at his mug. "I didn't deserve her."

My heart broke. "Oh. You did. I promise you."

Ethan shook his head. "No. I didn't. She was everything bright and wonderful, and I blew into her life and brought her darkness."

This was the most he'd ever shared. None of the Lords knew exactly what had happened to Ethan, and none had pried enough to find out. Some thought he had a wife; others thought he had a mate. Some said she died; some said she left. Ethan never spoke about his past, nor did he date that anyone knew of. I never saw any women visiting his Keep, other than shifters on business or the occasional mage.

I leaned forward. "No matter how much darkness is in someone's life, having such a love makes everything brighter. Cherish those moments and remember her during those times."

The light in his eyes began to dim.

"There's something between us. We both know it. But I'm done hoping for you to come around. I'll be a wonderful friend to you; the best you've ever had." I set my mug down and watched him. "Today is the last time you'll come into my home unannounced. If you want to see me, you call. You will no longer demand to know where I am or who I'm with." I let him see how serious I was. "If you do, our friendship will be over."

Ethan let out a heavy breath and scrubbed a hand through his hair. "Fuck."

My sentiments exactly. "I deserve better than this and you know it."

He rose and drained his mug. "Thank you for the tea."

I nodded. "You're welcome."

Ethan rinsed his mug out and set it on the side of the sink. When he turned around, his expression was unreadable. "I apologize for my behavior. It won't happen again."

"You are my friend, Ethan. If I can't have you in my life in the way I want, I'll take you how I can get you."

He looked down at his feet and exhaled.

"But you can't have the best of both worlds. It's unfair to me."

"I understand." When he lifted his head, his eyes were glowing again. "Evie said you were injured. Are you alright?"

I nodded. "Her dad took good care of me."

His jaw tightened at that, but he didn't demand to know exactly how he'd taken care of me. A step in the right direction as far as I was concerned.

"Is Soren alright?"

A flash of a grin brightened his face. "He's real pissed about the cat shifters, but they helped him deter the witches. He's good for now." His expression sobered. "Something happened there. Something big. Want to talk about it?"

I slowly shook my head. "The witches are going to be a bigger problem than we expected. I'm not entirely sure they're there for Soren."

His eyebrows lifted. "Oh?"

"Don't get me wrong. They definitely want to kill him and will happily make that a side quest, but I think their purpose is bigger than initially thought."

He scrubbed a hand over his jaw. "You're going back into his area?"

"Not for a day or two. I need rest and research. Does Soren have eyes on them?"

"Can't say. You need some?"

"Cernunnos told them they had to be off the territory by…" I grimaced. "Hours ago. If we lose them, I can't say for sure we'll find them again."

"I'll call Soren as soon as I leave. Get some rest. I'll text you when I hear something."

"Alright." My body was already urging me to curl up on the couch for a nap. The events of yesterday were catching up. I might have slept a full night last night, but released trauma takes a while for the physical body to heal. By tomorrow, I hoped to be up to full speed.

"Thanks, Ethan."

He nodded and walked to the door, turning once he opened it. "I won't stop taking care of you," he said quietly. "No demands, Moira. I promise. But I'll be damned if I see you suffer and do nothing."

"I'll do the same for you," I promised.

Ethan surprised me. I expected setting boundaries would end poorly, but the Lord had taken it well. Or, as well as a Lord could take someone putting their foot down.

"I don't like the thought of you taking a lover, Moira. Knowing someone else has their hands on you makes me want to tear the world apart."

I swallowed hard.

"But I hear what you're saying. As much as I hate to admit it, you're right. I will do my best to control my urges, but I suggest if you do take a lover, you shower before you visit."

Heat flamed my cheeks. "Ethan!"

His irises ringed with gold. "I know you didn't sleep with that god, but he had his hands on you for a lengthy amount of time. Whatever transpired between you two resulted in intimacy far greater than you've ever allowed him."

Before I could yell at him that it was none of his business, Ethan smiled. "You should know one more thing before I leave. Taking a lover won't get me out of your head, darling. And I want you to know anyone you take to your bed will never be able to satisfy you like I can."

"You—you tease!"

Ethan chuckled. "Maybe I'm just waiting for the right time."

I chucked my good mug right at his head, but he was too quick. Ceramic shattered against the sheetrock, putting a perfect circle dent in the wall.

The door shut on his soft laughter.

Arrogant ass.

CHAPTER

Fifteen

ETHAN

"You idiot," Rowan said fondly.

We sat around a campfire deep in the heart of his territory, only the wildlife to keep us company.

"You know why I can't," I growled.

He shook his head. "No. I know why you *won't*. There's a big difference."

There was no judgment in his tone or his eyes. I'd never told anyone about Sarah before Rowan, the pain still unbearable all these years later. She was the one thing I never wanted to share.

I selfishly hoarded all those memories with her, unwilling to speak about her with anyone, and resigned myself to living a long life alone. When I grew weary of immortality without her, I planned to go into the forest and lie down and die, opening myself up and gifting my life force to the earth.

And then I met Moira. We rarely spoke at first, and Soren had eyes on her. I had nothing to offer her and did my best to put her out of my mind.

Then the wench broke into my house and spied on me, her intoxicating scent permeating the entire house, and I found myself borderline obsessed.

Every time I was around her, I lost my damned mind.

"She's right," Rowan said gently.

"I know." Admitting it pissed me off. Waiting on her to come home had made me want to tear down her apartment. Smelling Cernunnos all over her skin made me want to sling Moira over my shoulder and imprint only my scent onto her soul. Dangerous thoughts and even more dangerous urges. She already carried my scent, but he'd washed most of it away. Whatever happened yesterday must have been intense for her to let him hold her like he had undoubtedly done.

Moira wasn't free with her affection. Not with me, not with Rowan's shifters. Only with Evie, Ash, and Tess, and even then, she hesitated to reach out. Something had happened to her in her past. I could smell it sometimes in her odd reactions to things.

The other Lord sighed and tossed an acorn into the fire. "I don't know Moira as well as Evie. Hell. No one does. The vampire is stingy with any information about herself. Sometimes I wonder if Evie realizes how closed off she is."

"She doesn't care," I said. "Moira would die for Evie, and she'd do the same for Moira."

"Friendship is funny like that," Rowan mused. "And so is love."

"I'm not in love with her," I muttered.

"Maybe not. But I remember how I felt every time I saw Evie with Caelan." He slid a look my way. "And my situation was admittedly worse."

I snorted. "Don't know how you stood that."

"Bears are patient, stealthy hunters, wolf. We can wait for long periods before we go in for the kill." Rowan grinned like a cat who'd gotten the canary.

The bastard had. He was mated and married and now the undisputed most powerful Shifter Lord in the world. Looking at him, you'd never know. He was the same Rowan he'd always been. Steady and patient and only violent when he needed to be.

Unlike the rest of us.

Guess being a bear had its perks sometimes.

"She says she wants to be my friend."

"Then be her friend."

I slid a look his way. "Is that how you got Evie?"

Rowan nodded. "You have to mean it, Ethan. If I had lied to Evie about being her friend, she would have figured me out and tossed me out on my ear. Rightfully so. I loved her enough to wait for her to be ready, and that meant being her friend. And only her friend."

I grunted. "Being friends with a woman is a novel concept."

"Rule one is keeping your hands to yourself. Open doors for her. Offer a hand to help her down the steps. A hand at the small of her back for pictures or escorting her inside. No intimate touches. No pushing her for something you aren't one hundred percent ready to give."

"She called me a tease." I'd laughed, but her words pissed me off because, once again, she was right. I *had* been teasing her.

"Careful," Rowan warned. "I've got a few dozen shifters who'd happily take her to bed. Push her far enough and she might take them up on the offer. You're lucky she hasn't done so already."

Rowan chuckled at the glow in my eyes. "You don't have the right to get angry at her over taking a lover if you aren't willing to be hers."

"Godsdammit, Rowan, I know. Doesn't mean I have to like it."

"You don't," he agreed, "but you better shut the fuck up if she does. Say nothing. Grit your teeth and bear it." Rowan tilted his face up to the sky. "My situation is extremely different from yours. If you aren't sure you'll ever be ready, you might be better off staying away from Moira for good."

I'd considered that, too. The thought of not seeing her again made something dark and ugly twist in my heart, but maybe it was for the best. Out of sight, out of mind and all that.

"She'd understand," Rowan said. "Moira is just as emotionally intelligent as Evie. They all are." He shook his head. "I've never seen such a group of different paranormals live in harmony like they have. Boggles the mind honestly."

"They're all good people who love each other. I have a few like them living on Keep grounds."

"Doesn't bother you?"

I shrugged. "Not at all. They contribute and keep their noses clean. Who am I to give a shit what branch of tree they're from?"

Rowan nodded. "I'm the same. There's a new fae in town I'm wondering about, though. She's got a talent with metal that makes my nose itch. Moira likes her. Evie likes her work. I wonder if she's going to bring trouble to my doorstep."

"What's her name?" I had contacts all over the world. If he was worried about her, it was better to know in advance who she was and if she had anything sketchy in her past.

"Ari Tavish."

"Nickname?"

He nodded. "I'll dig out her paperwork. If you can find anything out, I'd appreciate the help."

"No problem."

Rowan grinned. "And maybe having something to do with your time will keep you from sniffing around Moira's doorstep like a lost puppy."

"Asshole."

His bark of laughter dragged a reluctant smile to my face. Moira was a problem for me, but for tonight I could pretend like I was a normal guy spending outdoor time with a friend.

Maybe I could forget the unending pain in my heart for just a little while.

CHAPTER

Sixteen

Some lore claimed saying certain people's names out loud could summon them. Like Beetlejuice. Or Bloody Mary. My fingers hesitated over the top of my keyboard. Typing out my mother's fake name seemed like opening a door better left shut, but I had to know if she'd made a life in this country. I had to know who she was pretending to be.

The memories didn't feel as painful today. Talking to Cernunnos had ripped off the old scab of the wound, allowing them to heal just a little.

Two days of sleep and a Downton Abbey binge marathon made everything better, too.

I typed in *Minka Belyaev* and hit enter. The first page of results showed nothing. The name wasn't unusual, and knowing her, she'd planned it that way. I dug into the search results for a little while with mixed results. The image tab was less than helpful. Pictures weren't a thing when I was growing up, and I couldn't imagine she'd taken to them now, not when her proclivities could land her on the FBI's most wanted list.

I stumbled on an online apothecary. Innocent at first, but some of the herbs and supplies she carried had my eyebrows rising and piqued my interest. I remembered some of the same herbs in our home. How could I forget? Some of her worst punishments came inside her workroom, the smells of patchouli and valerian meshed in my brain so deeply my fingers hurt every time I smelled them.

She'd taken a hammer to them when I got my lessons wrong, smashing bone and cartilage, damaging my fingers so badly, even my vampiric healing couldn't keep up.

I shuddered and shoved the memories away.

Each page I flipped through tugged at me. I hit the Contact button and saw her name at the bottom. The About Us page had no pictures, but the bio was enough to make my stomach turn. This was her. It had to be.

I wrote down the address in the Notes area of my phone. She lived in the territory Evie had claimed. What were the odds of that?

I'd lived too long to believe in coincidences like that. After a few more fruitless searches, I shut my laptop down and went into the kitchen to scrounge something up for dinner, even though it was past nine p.m.

Tomorrow was a work day, and I had a shit ton of things to re-order so we didn't run out of supplies. The day after, I was off. I'd travel then and see if I could find Minka without being spotted.

If she was even still there.

My phone pinged.

Soren has eyes on the witches. They're out of his borrowed territory, but still in the area.

I frowned. Cernunnos might be interested to know they'd obeyed the spirit of his command but not the letter.

Are they still moving?

Yes. Right toward mine.

I chuckled.

How do you want me to respond?

I sent a thorough description of Minka and asked Soren to check if she was with them.

Intercept when they step into your territory and see what kind of info they're willing to give up on their reasons for being there.

Want me to kill them?

I laughed even knowing Ethan would if I asked him to.

Not yet. Approach with caution. I sent him the description of my mother.

My phone dinged with a message from Soren.

Negative. No witch by that description. Are you alright?

I'm fine, thank you. Heard you had some stray cats in your territory.

Fucking Cernunnos was his response.

Evie's dad was delightfully passive aggressive sometimes.

Be careful and keep it in your pants.

In typical Soren fashion, he responded with *How about I keep it in your pants?*, adding a wink emoji at the end.

Ignoring Soren, I sent one more text to Ethan. *Soren said the woman wasn't with them. If you see anyone matching her description, do not approach her.*

I tapped my fingers on the counter and fired off one more, knowing he'd have questions.

I'm serious. She might smell my presence and become curious.

Okay. That was a shitty way to explain Mom losing her ever-loving shit, but I wasn't ready to re-hash everything. Not with Ethan.

My phone rang, his name popping up on the screen.

I hit ignore. *Cooking. No time to talk.*

The phone rang again. I hit ignore once more.

Moira. Answer the phone.

Cooking.

He called one more time. I silenced my phone and went to the freezer to grab the ground beef.

Ethan called two more times before giving up.

My shoulders slumped with relief. I dumped the diced onion into the pot of browning ground beef and added a healthy amount of minced garlic, cumin, chili powder, salt, pepper, onion powder, a little Greek oregano, and a touch of dried habanero.

It might not be Tuesday, but it was definitely taco night.

I'd just finished rough chopping a shit ton of cilantro when the doorbell rang. The visitor's scent was obscured by all the spices and the simmering meat. "It's open!" I called, secure enough on Rowan's territory to know whoever was here meant no harm.

It was probably Evie.

"I'm making tacos if you want some!"

Ethan stepped into view. I blinked.

"I want," he said, his eyebrows lifting at the spread of fixings I had on the kitchen island.

"Oh. Umm. Sure."

He waved his cell at me. "You didn't answer. I tried to call before coming over. Because of your boundaries."

I pointed the knife at him. "How many of those potions do you have left?"

His eyes widened innocently. "Moira. I was already here."

"Lies," I grumbled. I'd given the Lord a supply of the travel potions during my time at his Keep. With the way he was blowing through them, he'd be out in a few weeks, which would stop him from popping onto Keep property every time I didn't answer the phone when he thought I should.

I stared at my pan of ground beef mixture and back at him. "You're hungry?"

He snorted. "I'm always hungry, and you know I love your tacos."

My heart warmed at his words. He did love my tacos and had hounded me to make them weekly when I stayed with him. If I'd known he'd pop in, I would have doubled the meat.

We hadn't seen each other or talked since our conversation. His absence hurt my heart, but having firm boundaries in place was good for both of us. I waved the knife at him. "I only made a pound and a half of meat, so you have to save me some."

He placed a hand on his heart. "I promise."

"Alright," I grumbled. "I'm almost finished."

I eyed the cheese grater and the chunk of cotija on the counter. "Want to grate that?" I gestured with the knife.

Ethan frowned at the contraption. "Mind showing me how to use that?"

I set my knife down and opened the top of the grater. "Put a chunk of cheese in that large enough for the top not to fit. Gently push the top back on and turn the handle."

Ethan nodded and took over, his eyes lighting up when the cotija came out finely grated. "Hell. I need to get one of these."

I snorted and went back to chopping the cilantro.

When he finished the cheese, he leaned over and took a sniff of the herb. "You didn't have that last time." He reached for a piece of the cilantro. I smacked his hand with the flat of the knife.

"No! You put it on the taco. It's a whole process."

Ethan stared at me wide-eyed. "Did you just smack me with a knife?"

"Cilantro is sacred."

"It's just a tiny piece."

"Yes, and it won't be nearly as delicious if you eat it by itself."

He sighed and plunked onto one of the kitchen stools. "Fine. Tutor me in the fine art of tacos, Moira."

"Don't be a smart ass."

Ethan chuckled and took a hunk of the cheese. "You didn't have this either."

A curious look crossed his face. "What is this?"

"Cotija."

"I like it."

"Good because that's how tacos should be."

"Why didn't you have this at the house?"

I eyed him. "Has no one ever made you real tacos before?"

His eyes darkened for a brief moment, making me wonder if I overstepped. "No," he finally said.

"You live in the middle of nowhere. Sourcing ingredients like this is difficult in remote places." I pointed to the cilantro. "I grew this in the courtyard garden, and the cheese came from the shop downtown."

His eyes narrowed. "If you wanted things like this, why didn't you say something?"

"Because I could still make tacos without them. Trying to find these specific ingredients might not have been easy." I frowned. "Well, the cilantro might not have been too difficult, but the cheese would."

"Rowan has a cheese guy?"

"A woman. And they didn't have cotija either until I made a specific request. Sometimes I cook for the Pack, so it's worth her carrying it because you know what it's like cooking for shifters. She makes a month's worth of rent just on the cotija we order."

Ethan grunted. "I wonder how hard it would be to get a cheese guy."

I laughed. "You don't have a downtown area. Not really. Might not be worth the effort."

"Do you want cotija when you're at the Keep?"

I set my knife down and studied him. "Are you inviting me back?"

His dark eyes warmed. "Darling, I never wanted you to leave."

I scoffed even as my blood heated. "Your Pack was starting to get weird."

"So?"

"I'm a vampire."

"Sort of."

"Ethan," I groaned. "We were spending too much time together, and your shifters were starting to ask uncomfortable questions. You started getting weird."

He crossed his arms over his chest. "And yet, I didn't ask you to leave."

"You should have. I did what was best for both of us."

Ethan's eyes narrowed. "Alright then. If that hadn't happened, how long would you have stayed?"

I would have stayed forever, even knowing he'd never care about me like I did him. "No idea."

My pause was too long. Satisfaction gleamed in Ethan's eyes. "I see," he murmured. "Interesting."

"There's nothing interesting about this. I'm back home and have no plans to leave."

The oven timer went off. Screaming a mental thank you at the good timing, I grabbed the pot holder and took the shells out, while hoping Ethan would drop the subject.

I had a wonderful time at his Keep. I loved his people; I loved the wild remoteness of his territory. I loved sitting outside watching deer and eagles and all the animals Ethan prevented his people from hunting. I loved the garden I built and maintained.

If I went back, my heart would slowly break.

"Come back."

His voice was low and rough and sent the hair on the back of my neck. I took the lid off the meat, set it aside, and gave the beans one more stir. "Help yourself."

"Moira."

I put five taco shells on a plate and handed it to him. "Boundaries, Ethan."

He sighed and took the plate. "We're not done with this conversation."

"Meat first. Then beans. Then all the fixings."

He eyed me. "And then the cilantro?"

"Start with a little and see how you like it." I grabbed the other plate and started making mine, shoving a shit load of cilantro on top when I was finished.

His eyebrows lifted. "Is that a normal amount of that stuff?"

"Nope," I said happily and plopped onto the living room couch.

Ethan came in a little while later. I'd already turned the television on, hoping we could stay away from the heavy topics tonight.

When he reached over and turned the volume down, I had to stifle my sigh.

"I don't want to talk about this. You know why I left."

"This isn't about the Keep. Tell me what's going on with Soren and the witches. Everything. Something happened to you there."

I crunched into my taco and chewed long enough for him to roll his eyes. We dug in and ate in blissful silence for a while. Ethan got up after finishing his first taco and added more cilantro to his others.

"You're awfully bossy." Cernunnos encouraged me to talk about what happened. Doing so felt like trying to exercise an atrophied muscle.

"I care about you. If there's something wrong, I'd like to know about it, so I can help you."

"I don't need help."

He took a bite of his taco and watched me.

I thought about it. Ethan had a lot of connections I didn't. He might be able to help me more than I could help myself.

"It's that woman, isn't it? The one you told me to stay away from."

"This conversation stays between you and me."

Ethan put his plate down and got up to rummage in my cabinets.

"What are you doing?"

"You got any of Cliona's booze?"

I snorted. "Yes. Why?"

"This sounds like we might need some."

"Left hand cabinet. I like her flavored vodkas but get whatever you want."

Ethan made us both a drink, flavored vodka tonics, and plunked one down before me.

"First, darling, anything you ever tell me about yourself stays right in the vault. Second, this woman did something to you, didn't she?"

I took a fortifying sip of my drink and began to tell the story.

CHAPTER

Seventeen

ETHAN

Shifters need time to learn how to manage their emotions and aggression, which is why we're never left alone once we reach the time around our first shift. Puberty and magic do not mix well. Left to our own devices, a single shifter can wreak complete and total havoc in a town.

Even after we get through puberty and become an adult—a viable and responsible member of a Pack inside a Keep, keeping your emotions in check is always an exercise in mental fortitude.

Moira wasn't telling me everything. I felt the knowledge deep in my bones. But the little she was telling me sent rage bubbling through my bloodstream. The urge to rip and tear and shred pumped within me, Moira's shaky, hesitant voice strengthening my urges until her words were drowned out with the rage of my wolf.

The woman—her mother—had to die. She'd hurt Moira. Over and over and over again, then forced her into a transformation she never wanted so she could hurt her even more. Claws slid from my fingers. Light from my eyes sent a golden wash over the room.

Cool fingers touched my cheeks. "Ethan."

A warm body pressed into me, Moira's skin against mine.

"Ethan. Come back to me."

Her gentle voice and her skin against mine made me want so badly for something I didn't deserve. Not after her—

She stroked her fingers down my jaw, her dark hair sliding against my neck. "Ethan," she whispered once more.

My hands cupped her face. Moira went still, her wide, almost black eyes locked onto mine. Her heart pounded, and I smelled the blood rushing through her veins.

"She hurt you." I barely recognized my voice.

Moira swallowed. "Yes."

"So many times."

Tears swam in her eyes. "It's been over for many years. I've lived entire lifetimes since then."

"Running from her but never entirely free."

Moira didn't respond, but we both knew the answer. I ran a hand down the smooth skin of her neck and picked up a handful of hair, allowing the silky strands to glide through my fingers. "Are you going to kill her?"

Moira closed her eyes, tilting her face into my palm. "Not sure I can."

I snorted, finally beginning to come back to myself. She was in my lap facing me, her knees on either side of my hips. We were far closer than we'd ever been before.

Moira realized it at the same time I did. She drew back, mumbling an apology.

I put my hands around her hips. "Moira."

She went still. "I didn't think. I'm sorry."

Moira's eyes were downcast and her body had gone stiff.

"You think I don't want you, but I can assure you nothing is further from the truth."

I gently pressed her hips down, so she'd make full contact with me.

Her mouth opened in a slight "oh" of surprise when she felt exactly what her presence was doing. Heat turned her cheeks pink. The scent of her desire filled the air.

My hands slid up her back. I leaned forward, so close her breath brushed against my skin.

"Don't do this and walk away. I don't think I can bear it."

I captured her lips with my own.

CHAPTER
Eighteen

When I thought of Ethan, I always thought of ice. He was cold and calculating and sometimes even cruel.

Tonight, he was fire. His hands were warm against my back. His lips firm and unyielding, gentle and exploratory. He tasted of cumin and spice.

I didn't do anything for a long moment, knowing he'd come to his senses and pull away, and I didn't want to seem too eager or rush anything. The Lord was powerful but fragile, and I wouldn't do anything to hurt him.

To my surprise, he did neither. His fingers tangled in my hair, and he leaned back, taking me with him. I melted against his body and opened my mouth. His tongue slid inside, eliciting an involuntary moan of surrender from me. He smelled of pine and wild things and the seasonings I'd used for dinner, and that should have been weird, but all I could think of was how much Ethan felt like home.

My hands slid up his chest, exploring the lean planes of his muscles, stopping to cup his face. Ethan deepened the kiss, turning it into something savage and raw. Desire flooded my body. The urge to rip his clothes off tore at my mind, the need to claim him pounding in my head. It took everything I had not to respond to the voice in my head telling me to undress him, take him to my bed and make him mine.

Any moment, he would come to his senses and realize it was me he was touching, me he was kissing. Not the woman he loved with everything he was.

I wasn't her. I'd never be her.

"Stop thinking," he murmured against my lips.

I pulled back and eyed him. "Are you alright?"

Ethan's rumbling chuckle made my stomach flip. "A beautiful woman just fed me dinner and made out with me a little. The night would be perfect, but she stopped and asked me if I was alright."

I shoved his chest gently. "Ass."

I tried to get off his lap, but his hands held me firm. "I'm fine."

I must have looked doubtful. Ethan's lips tipped into a small smile. "Maybe I'll regress when I get home. No way to know. For now, I am here with you, and everything is right with the world. Instead of overthinking things, can we sit here tonight, together, and just be?"

I blinked the moisture in my eyes away. "Yes." My voice was husky. "Of course."

Six months ago, he would have run away. No. Scratch that. He never would have let me crawl onto his lap or touch him. We'd turned a corner tonight. Where it would take us was anyone's guess.

But for tonight, I could do exactly as he asked.

Eventually, when I started whining about still being hungry, Ethan let me off his lap. I dished out the rest of the tacos and handed Ethan his half. He patted the seat next to him.

When I eyed him, he snorted. "Come sit beside me. Please."

He didn't have to tell me twice. I curled against him and we ate together, a companionable silence taking up the space between us.

I'd eaten with him before. Many times. But tonight there was a comfortable intimacy not present before. I liked it. I liked this.

And after tonight's kiss, I was half convinced I was in love with him.

I shoved that thought down deep into the cold metal box inside my heart I rarely opened. Tonight was a memory I'd cherish forever, but I wasn't foolish enough to think this would last. Not with Ethan always running hot and cold. Tonight was the hottest he'd ever been, allowing a small sliver of hope to catch in my heart. Tomorrow might bring an attack of conscience and reverse all our progress.

But tonight, I was curled against him, warm and content, sharing a drink and talking. And that was worth more than all the bad moments we'd had together.

I DRIFTED off to sleep on accident and woke up with a start. Heat warmed my skin, making my brow furrow until I remembered where I was and who was with me. Sometime during the night, he'd lain down and took me with him. His arm was wrapped around my waist, his breath tickling my hair. I closed my eyes and soaked in his warmth. As soon as he woke up, things would be different.

There's something about darkness allowing people to be who they truly are. Daylight was when the masks returned. I had a hundred things I needed to do. His arms tightened around me and he shifted, bringing me closer against him.

Those things could wait.

Ethan's posture went stiff an hour or so later. Sadness filled me when his hand left my waist. I sat up and moved away from him, giving him a moment to get his bearings.

He watched me as I busied myself with making a pot of coffee and putting the kettle on. I said nothing as I worked. When I had both drinks in hand, I handed him the coffee and took my London fog latte over to the recliner where I curled up and watched him.

His eyes held regret, and that was worse than anything else.

"Good morning," I murmured.

"Moira—"

"There's no need," I interrupted. "I knew last night this wouldn't last. Don't ruin the memory, please."

His nostrils flared. Ethan reached for the mug. "Thank you."

I nodded and blew on my tea.

We sat in silence for a while, and my eyes kept drifting to the Lord on my couch. He was already a handsome man, but rumpled Ethan with wrinkled clothes and five-o'clock shadow, and his hands curled around my favorite mug?

That Ethan was devastating.

Desire heated my blood once more, forcing me to squash the emotion down and beat it into submission. I needed to find a boyfriend, a lover—anyone to help me forget this man or at least numb the edges of my feelings toward him.

"Why are you looking at me like that?" Ethan rumbled.

I shrugged. "Just thinking."

His eyes narrowed. "About?"

"Don't worry about it."

Ethan's fingers tightened around the mug. "Moira—"

"Ethan. Don't. You did nothing I didn't expect. Let's just drop it, okay?"

He blew out a breath. "Fine. Are you going to look for your mother today?"

"Haven't decided yet."

"She wasn't with those other witches. Maybe she's long gone."

"Doubtful. Evie attracted a lot of attention with her dealings last year, and I was heavily involved. Mom wouldn't risk attacking a Keep, but I bet she knows I'm here. She's biding her time." Like a snake in the grass waiting for a meal.

"I'll come with you."

I smiled at Ethan, knowing it didn't reach my eyes. Inside I felt weary and a little heartsick. "No. I'm not doing anything today other than scoping out one of her properties. If she isn't there, I'll look around town and ask a few questions."

"I'll go with you," he said again.

"No." I set my mug down. "I think it's best if we don't see each other as much."

Ethan's jaw set, a ring of gold appearing around his irises. "I disagree."

It wasn't even nine in the morning and I was already annoyed. "I enjoy spending time with you."

"Good. Then let's do that all the time."

I gave him an exasperated look. "I deserve to have someone in my life who doesn't pull away when things get real or intimate. Don't you think so?"

His exhale was heavy. "I need time."

I spread my hands out. "Then take it."

The way he watched me made my heart break a little. "And what will you do?"

"What anyone else would. Live my life."

"And date?"

"If I did?"

"I don't want you to," he growled.

"You can't have it both ways," I said gently.

When he opened his mouth, I held up a hand. "I know you aren't ready. Last night was wonderful, but I knew when we woke up this morning, we'd be right here having a discussion like this. You give a little then take it all away." I shook my head. "This is my fault, actually."

Ethan blinked. "Pardon?"

"I should have shut the door on you yesterday. Kept it where we left it."

The flicker of hurt in his eyes almost made me stop, but he had to hear this. I had to get the words out. "We were civil and borderline friendly. Now there's this tension in the air between us. I can't stand it." Tears burned my eyes. "I don't deny that I care about you more than I should, and I think you know it, too. I even suspect you care about me a little, too. But you'd be lying to yourself if you told me you were ready for more. I can see it in your eyes, read it in your skin. Last night, for the first time, I held a tiny sliver of hope in my heart for us, but I woke up this morning, and I knew whatever magic we'd captured would be gone once you woke up."

"How could you have known something like that?"

I wasn't psychic. Nothing of the sort. Women's intuition was almost like a hive mind, a set of learned experiences genetically encoded into female DNA and passed down to every generation. Sometimes, we just knew. Even if every single clue or happening told us otherwise.

"I wasn't wrong, was I?"

His jaw tightened. "Have I ever told you how much I dislike how eloquently you communicate?"

I wasn't sure how to respond. "Thank Evie for that. She always said no one is going to know how you feel about things if you don't open your mouth and tell them."

Ethan shook his head. "Sounds like something she'd say."

"Well, it took her a while to get there." When Evie and I first met, we circled around each other warily for a long time. It took years to get to know her. Even now, she held her tongue if something didn't directly impact her, but if it did, get ready to hear an earful.

Ethan finished his coffee. "Once again, you're right."

"I'm well aware."

He smiled, a tinge of sadness in the gesture. "I'll get out of your hair this morning. Thanks for the tacos."

Ethan stood and glanced at the couch, lingering on the spot where we laid together. "And the long nap."

"Take care of yourself."

He nodded. "Sure you don't want some company today?"

"I'm a vampire." I wiggled my fingertips. "With claws and everything. Thanks for the offer, but I'll be fine."

A few minutes later he was gone. I sank into my seat and closed my eyes. Every time he left, my heart gained a new crack. Few relationships were easy. They weren't meant to be. There were always kinks to work out and quirks to either accept or walk away from. Whatever this was between us was a whole lot more than smoothing out some edges.

Starting today, though, I had to think about myself. I cared about Ethan, but this was his trauma to work through, and I couldn't let him keep hurting me while he tried to figure things out. The next time he knocked, I wouldn't let him inside. Keeping him at arm's length was the only way I could get over him.

Once I finished my tea and got dressed, I went into my spell room and dug through my potion supply, making a mental note to refresh all my materials the second I had extra time. The last thing I needed was to run out of something important right when I was in a pinch.

I tucked two of the ever popular travel potions inside my oversized purse, careful to wrap them in soft cloth and a protective case first. Nothing else stood out to me, so I took a quick look at my herb supply and jotted down a few things to purchase in town when I got back.

Snacks were second on the list. I tossed a plastic baggie of Evie's famous granola and some of Rowan's experimental jerky inside the bag. Rowan was hit or miss in the kitchen, and I hadn't yet tried the jerky.

But it was jerky. Was it possible to screw up dried-within-an-inch-of-its-life meat? I'd find out in a little while, I guess.

Once I had all my supplies, I headed out the door only to see Cernunnos sitting in one of my patio chairs.

He was sipping something steaming from one of Evie's favorite ceramic mugs. "Heading out?" he asked.

I stopped and blinked. "Uh. You could have knocked?"

"Didn't want to interrupt. Need a ride?"

"You hate transporting people. In fact, I'm pretty sure you retired from it because, and I quote, 'you assholes need to learn how to drive.' Or something like that."

A faint smile touched his lips. "Evie is finally comfortable with her skills in that department. She can tote her shifters among all the realms if she wishes now."

"And you're freelancing?" He was making me suspicious. The god had saved our asses a few times and been pretty helpful over the past couple of years, but Cernunnos always had an ace up his sleeve.

"Something like that." He jerked his head. "I know you have potions in your purse, but why waste them? Tell me where you're going and I'll be happy to escort you."

I crossed my arms over my chest. "Why?"

He laughed and spread his hands out. "What answer would please you? Because I am curious? Because I have an agenda?"

"The truth would be nice." The fae played fast and loose with the truth, but someone like him had a way of mixing it with lies so well it might ruin your life if you took anything he said at face value.

"What can I say? I'm immortal and you are interesting."

Alright. Maybe too much truth was a bad thing sometimes.

He chuckled at my sour expression but set his mug down and stood, his face sobering. "I know where you're going today. If anything, you will save two of those precious potions and have a god as backup in case things go awry."

Ethan would give me so much shit if he knew I turned him down only to say yes to Cernunnos less than an hour later.

"If you're good, I'll take you to visit Ember."

"Dammit." Who could resist an adorable fox? "Fine. Let me put this back inside the house. Are you ready to go?"

He rolled his eyes. "I'll wait for you here. Don't be too long."

I kept the snacks and put the potions back. He was waiting for me in the yard, staring up at the dormitories. Even knowing who he was, Rowan's shifters weren't quite comfortable with his presence on their land. Few spoke to him unless they had to, but Declan spotted him and was making his way over.

I was too far away to hear what they spoke about, but whatever Declan said was brief and made Cernunnos smile. They shook hands and parted ways just as I came upon them. Declan nodded, eyes twinkling with amusement. "Safe travels. Want me to tell Evie you're leaving?"

He didn't add "with Evie's dad," but we both knew he was thinking it. "If you want to. I'll text her later, though."

I had to text the shop employees and let them know I'd be out today but in tomorrow. My help wasn't quite up to the quality Evie had when she first got involved with the Lords. Mine weren't quite family, nor was I sure they'd ever get there.

Declan nodded and turned to walk away. Cernunnos nodded at the Second's back. "I like him. He is powerful but secure in who he is. Rowan will never have to worry about a challenge with him."

Declan and I weren't friends, but I liked him. "I'd be more scared of Evie than Rowan."

Cernunnos grinned. "True. Her selection of mates was surprisingly gentle."

He held out his hand. "Where are we going, gods-touched?"

I held the image in my mind and took his hand. His palm was rough and calloused and warmer than a shifter's, a fact I'd never noticed before. "Not too close. I don't want to risk her seeing me."

"Keep your eyes closed and do not let go."

In a sickening lurch, we were off.

For a small town in Montana, the town square was surprisingly bustling. People milled in and out of stores holding multiple shopping bags. We landed on a roof two buildings to the left and on the opposite side of the store I was surveilling.

"Down," Cernunnos murmured. "Humans don't look up, but others do. We're sticking out like sore thumbs up here."

We ducked and hurried over to the edge of the roof, finding a spot to help conceal us. Cernunnos waved a hand. "There. We can move about as much as we wish now."

"You could have done that when we landed."

"I needed a moment to get my bearings. Use too much magic, and it will bring attention."

"Thank you."

"Your thanks sound a little grumpy, Moira."

I eyed him. "You don't have to stay, you know."

He laid a hand over his heart. "How you wound me. Of course I'll stay. It's been ages since I've been on a proper stakeout."

"If anything, this would be considered mild stalking."

"You're gathering intel on a criminal. Stalking is a crime of power. You have no desire to control the woman or actually see her other than to find out her movements so you can stop her."

"Hmm. Stakeout," I mused. "I like it."

"Good. Now all we need is junk food and too much coffee."

"I'm afraid I have neither of those." I pointed at my bag. "Snacks in there. No coffee."

He wiggled his fingers. "Have you forgotten? I'm magical."

"No coffee. Because I am not magical and neither is my bladder."

I sat cross-legged on the ground. "Now hush. I need to focus."

Root and Branch, the name of my mother's apothecary, had a surprisingly cute storefront. The sign above the shop had a dark wooden background with lighter wooden letters in a stylized font. Oak leaves twined around the R and B in the name.

The shop did a brisk business. People milled in and out, human and witch alike, most exiting the store with at least one bag. I could only assume she sold more than herbs inside, as some of the bags were larger than I was used to seeing come out of a shop like that.

We sat there for a few hours, Cernunnos occasionally making cracks about certain people. "I wish I knew if she's there today," I murmured.

"It's almost lunch. Maybe she'll come out to take her break."

"Dunno," I said offhandedly. "I'm sure she's holding at least two people captive in her basement to snack on."

A warm hand settled on my shoulder at the moment I realized what I'd said. If he hadn't known what happened to me, maybe he would have laughed. "We'll wait," he said quietly.

I glanced up. "Is this why you came? You felt sorry for me?"

"I'm too ancient to feel sorry for anyone, Moira." He sank down beside me and crossed his legs. "I came because I did not want a friend to face the thing that haunts them alone."

Tears burned the backs of my eyes. My throat clogged. I looked away and nodded. "Thank you," I croaked.

"Tell me one happy thing you remember from your childhood."

I kept my eyes on the apothecary's entrance while I thought about it. "There was a stray dog in town. He was brown and black and white and had the floppiest ears I'd ever seen."

"Some type of hound," Cernunnos remarked.

"Maybe. Larger than a beagle and had a barrel chest but wasn't a Basset."

I called him Scout, which was a typical name for a dog back then. He wasn't mine. I would never dare to bring a living thing into my mother's household. Every time I saw him, he'd come up and show his belly, but oddly enough, he never came out when my mother was with me, almost as if he knew the unlimited bounds of her cruelty.

"I always brought a flask of water with me to share. We'd go into the forest for as long as I could and sit there. He put his head in my lap and snoozed."

"Sounds like a good memory."

"It was. We moved a few years later. Asking my mother to take him with us would have signed his death warrant." A memory I hadn't thought of in years struck me. "The wildlife stopped visiting us the week we moved in. No birds sang in the trees. No bugs or snakes skittered along the ground. Every place we moved into had an emptiness about it."

"Animals have far keener senses than we do sometimes."

"I'd forgotten how much I missed those sounds until I saw my mother again." I pushed my legs out in front of me. "Evie has always had life reaching for her, and I took comfort in all the plant life surrounding us. But it's not the same as having an animal companion."

"No," Cernunnos agreed. "It is not."

"Do you have one that hangs around?" I glanced over at him.

Cernunnos watched the door as closely as I was. "They're around me constantly," he admitted. "I have to ask for a moment of peace if I need one."

"Pets are frowned on at the Keep. Too many children now."

Cernunnos snorted. "Evie's Rowan is worried about their pets getting eaten?"

I laughed. "Evie more so than Rowan. Shifters can't control their instincts for many years. And eating a pet will traumatize everyone, so the general rule is not to bring one around."

"What about Ethan's Keep?"

My eyes narrowed. "What about it?"

He grinned, those ancient eyes swirling with amusement. "I smelled him all over your apartment this morning."

He didn't have to say "and you."

Shit. Sometimes I forgot how well paranormals could smell. I'm not sure why. I was one of them. I guess I just forgot when it concerned me. Mostly because I didn't make a habit of snuggling Shifter Lords on my couch.

"I'm assuming Ethan's Keep is the same way. My dreams of pet ownership are on hold until I decide to get my own place."

"Have you thought about moving out?"

"I like being close to Evie." And hated being alone.

Cernunnos went still. "Watch."

I leaned forward, peering at the door. Two people came out, neither of whom were my mother.

I started to relax, but the door opened once more. Minka, as she called herself now, was taller than me by a couple of inches. She had the same dark hair as I did, but her eyes were the true green of a pureblood witch. Mine were so dark, they looked black in certain light. She always called my eyes muddy and blamed my father for ruining our bloodline.

Seemed she never thought she might have participated in that.

Today, her hair was arranged in a neat chignon, a few strands loosened to soften the sharp angles of her face. She wore a pair of taupe, wide-legged flowing pants, a white tank top, and a colorful kimono cardigan on top. Her gaze swept the street, a furrow appearing on her perfect brow.

I started to shrink back. Cernunnos put a hand on my arm. "Trust, Moira. She cannot see us."

"But she senses something here."

"Perhaps," he said, studying my mother intently. "Power calls to power."

"You think she's powerful?"

"She has stolen the life force from thousands," he said roughly. "Her power comes from stolen magic. My answer is yes, she will be formidable to challenge, but not invincible." His eyes began to swirl. "I will instruct the local fauna to stay far from her. They probably already will, but it takes a while for darkness to seep into the land. It's safest for them to avoid her entirely. As her sacrifices dry up, her magic will weaken."

I stared at him for a moment. "That's smart."

"I should hope so. I've been alive since the dawn of time, Moira. If I hadn't learned anything since then, I'd be afraid for my very soul."

What must it be like to be connected with every living thing? Evie was similar, but she was more connected to flora than fauna. All I imagined was a web of interconnection with him at the center. "Tell Ember, please," I said, thinking of what might happen to him if Mom spotted him close to where she was performing magic. "I know he won't be out this way, but in case he is, I don't want anything to happen to him."

Cernunnos smiled. "You are fond of the little fox."

"How could I not be? He's adorable, and he likes me, so obviously he's perfect."

My mom got into a sleek BMW and started to pull out of the parking lot.

"Shit. How can we follow?" I must be off my game. Her leaving had never occurred to me. Ethan. I gritted my teeth. Every time he was around, my brain became scrambled eggs.

The god held out his hand. "Come. I will show you a trick or two."

Minka pulled out of the parking lot. Cernunnos tugged me

along, the world flashing by in a rainbow of colors. I sucked in a stunned breath and followed. We were running but not. Somehow, we moved through a stream of time and events, everything in fast forward. Keeping an easy pace with the car, Cernunnos stayed several feet back to keep her from sensing us, I assumed.

After a while, she pulled into the parking lot of a cute rental home with dark blue shutters. There wasn't a lick of landscaping or flowers within five feet around the home, and most of the grass had died.

She'd been living there for a while now, based on the lack of green things.

Cernunnos slowed and pulled us into the dense woods across the street. "Wait."

Minka got out of the car and went inside. The day was still early. Odds were she wasn't home for the rest of the day. If she left again, we could get inside and try to find out what she was planning.

She wouldn't leave her territory undefended. Even now, I could sense her dark power shimmering around the house and parts of the yard. The place had to be rigged with traps.

"Do you think we can get inside?"

Cernunnos narrowed his eyes. "Dead things live inside, gods touched. I don't think you want to go in there."

I closed my eyes. "Human?"

Cernunnos didn't answer for a moment until he noticed my attention. "Human, shifter. Other animals." He let out a heavy sigh. "I am sorry you were exposed to her, Moira. My offer to kill her still stands."

As we stood there, I strongly considered ending things right then. My mother would stand no chance against a god.

Cernunnos could go in and kill her where she stood, ending my eternal nightmare for good.

"Allow me to do this for you," he said quietly.

I always liked how Cernunnos didn't clean up other people's messes. He let Evie fight her own battles, for the most part, and only stepped in where he felt he could do the most good. If I told him no, he might not like it, but he would stay his hand.

I said nothing for a long moment. She'd done unspeakable things to me, forced me into an immortality I never wanted so she could keep me as a victim, and the only reason I got away was because I planned for years and finally made my move when she was out of town.

I'd been running ever since.

My head was nodding before I could stop myself.

Cernunnos's nostrils flared. "Yes?"

"Yes," I whispered.

Power punched through the air, visceral and raw, leaving the real Cernunnos standing before me, a god of such immense power I could barely look at him. His antlers loomed above his head, those strange eyes swirling with multicolored magic.

"Stay here," he commanded and disappeared.

I regretted the decision immediately. Sending him in when he couldn't know what kind of monster she was seemed cruel to me.

A high-pitched female scream rang out. All the windows in the house shattered.

"Shit." I left my hiding place and approached the house, carefully skulking around the edge.

Minka's dark magic mixed with emerald green and silver, grunts of effort, both feminine and male, trickled through the windows. I slowly rose up and looked inside.

Minka and Cernunnos faced off, both of their hands raised in defensive positions. My mother was brutally injured, half her face burned and twisted. Cernunnos had punched a hole in her side, large enough to fit a handbag through.

And yet, she was still standing.

A chill rolled down my spine. She should be dead. Why wasn't she dead?

"What could I have done to a god?" Minka asked.

Cernunnos loomed over her. "There are no living creatures here. You've taken too much of my natural bounty."

Minka's eyes narrowed. "No." She shook her head. "You lie. Your animals die every day, by hands crueler than mine could ever be."

A shield bubbled between them. "Tell me, god, does that woman you were with have anything to do with this?"

"Make your peace with the world, witch."

Minka laughed, the sound rasping. "You underestimate my power, god. I've always wanted to tangle with one such as you." She clicked her tongue. "Though you are a fine male specimen. Perhaps instead of tangling together in conflict, we should entwine in a more pleasurable way."

Oh. Ick. No matter how much I hated my mother, hearing her proposition any man got my gag reflexes up.

Cernunnos laughed. My shoulders fell with relief. "You will never sully me with your touch, witch."

Power snapped through the air. I ducked down and waited.

Minka's power had always felt cold and oily to me, like someone had switched the butter for shortening in icing. An odd way to think about dark magic, but hers felt like a betrayal. Much like a baker who used shortening in their buttercream.

Speaking of which…I was going to make Cernunnos a big ass cake when we got out of here.

Just as I was growing concerned, the house rocked with a stunning boom of power. The siding I leaned against bucked, throwing me several feet into the air. Black smoke curled with emerald and silver poured from the shattered windows.

I landed with a hard slam against the ground, the breath knocked out of me.

Stunned, I blinked a few times, trying to catch my breath.

Silence reigned, and as I slowly got to my feet, the house began to crack and groan. There was no way she was still alive. I slipped behind a tree on the other side of the property and waited.

More smoke poured from the house. Concern brimmed in my veins. I stepped out from my hiding spot just as a flash of blinding light snapped from the windows and a body slammed through the wall like a comet.

It wasn't my mother.

"Fuck," I breathed as I took off running.

Fumbling through my bag, I swore as I realized I'd left those travel potions at my apartment. I landed beside Cernunnos's still form and gently shook.

"You have to wake up," I whispered. "We'll die here if we stay."

I gently lifted him, and settled him half in my lap, my arms under his upper back. If he woke up, I'd be touching him and he could get us out faster.

The back door fell off the hinges, revealing a dark-haired woman covered in soot and blood. She stepped onto the porch, her vivid gaze sweeping the area until it landed on me.

Realization settled on her face. "I knew there was something familiar about the woman he was with," she said. Her accent was less pronounced than it used to be, but she was the same woman who'd made my life a living hell.

She studied me for a long moment. "You're a woman now."

"Too old for you."

Minka snorted. "Life force is life force, my darling. While a child's is more potent, it all becomes the same energy in the end."

"Wake up, please," I whispered to Cernunnos. He was breathing, I knew that much, but his chest was a ruin.

Minka stepped off the porch and walked toward me.

"Stay away," I croaked, disgusted by the same shiver of fear I felt as a child.

She clicked her tongue. "I am your mother, and we have not seen each other for so very long. Surely you will not begrudge me a visit."

How was she still upright? Her chest was a smoking ruin.

She caught my gaze. "Ah. It will heal within the hour. My spell work is much more powerful than it used to be."

Minka came closer.

"I am not without my own power, Mother. Do not take one more step."

"Och," she chided. "Has my kitten grown claws, then?"

My stomach filled with acid. She only called me that when she wanted something, the term of endearment poison on her lips.

"You should have stayed hidden, my dear." Her teeth were streaked with crimson, the cavernous ruin of her chest seeping blood. "The witches were easy enough to manipulate. They wanted the Lord too badly to understand the cost of my help."

Things clicked into place. She must be feeding from the witches' life force. Made sense if she survived Cernunnos coming after her.

"Stay there," I barked when she took another step.

Minka heeded my warning. She hesitated, unsure what I might be able to do to her. Vampires had a stable of powers, but much like the Lords, all of them had one special gift. Some could mesmerize anything that breathed. Others could fly. Some had invisibility.

Few spoke about their unholy powers.

I had one. If I revealed my gift, Cernunnos might be conscious enough to remember what I could do.

If I didn't, we both might die.

The god's fingers twitched. He licked his lips. Keeping a careful eye on Minka, I bent closer.

"Drink," he whispered, so low only I could hear him.

My eyes snapped to him. "No."

"I do not have enough power to move us. You must."

Tears filled my eyes. "How?" How could I have known what I was or what I could do?

"Drink," he commanded.

I saw no other way out. My mother took a few cautious steps forward, her eyes narrowing as she strained to listen.

"Cernunnos..."

He grimaced in pain as he tilted his neck. My mother took another step closer.

Running out of time, I dipped my head and struck like a viper.

CHAPTER
Twenty

ost vampires made their bites pleasurable. I had no time to do so. My teeth sank into the warm skin of his neck, and I drank as much as I could without further weakening him. Cernunnos's blood slammed into me, magic humming through every cell in my body. He was consummate power, divine energy. I'd never tasted anything like his blood. Ripping my mouth away before I got too distracted by his taste, I stumbled to my feet.

The ground rumbled underneath my feet.

Minka stopped walking. She let out a startled laugh. "Fool. He will kill you for your trespass."

She had no idea he'd given me permission.

"What are you doing with a god anyway? I thought I taught you not to involve yourself in their schemes. Nothing good ever comes by doing so."

More magic than I'd ever had in my life filled every part of me. Cernunnos's power was life, green and wild things. I could feel the earth quivering beneath my feet, sense every single living thing within the soil. Animals, hidden behind trees and in deep brush, carefully watched us.

With this much power, there was no way my mother could have beaten him. She must have taken him by surprise.

"Stop." My voice had changed, became deeper and more authoritative.

Minka snorted. "You might be a little faster than me high on that blood you've taken, little girl, but I put a god on his knees. Make this easier and come with me willingly. I do not wish to harm you."

I couldn't help myself. I laughed. The statement sounded so absurd coming from her. Of course she wanted to hurt me. That's what someone like her did.

Dark, viscous magic swirled from my mother, a heartbeat before she reached out her hand and threw a spell meant to incapacitate. I knew that spell. She'd done it to me hundreds of items.

I stepped out of the way with ease, the spell flying past to sink harmlessly into the ground. In the past, I would have frozen in terror. Mom's eyes narrowed, displeasure sparking in the green depths.

I didn't give her the opportunity to try again. Flinging both hands, I threw every bit of power I could. Magic slammed into her, tossing her ass over teakettle for several feet. Minka smashed into the side of the house, so surprised, she failed to make any sound besides a bark of pain when she hit the wood.

I ran back to Cernunnos, skidding on my knees to land beside him. "Wake up." I gently smacked him on the cheek.

He grunted. "Recovering."

Mom groaned and tried to get to her feet.

"For fuck's sake," I growled. "Why won't you die?"

"Unholy power," Cernunnos whispered. "Something else fuels her. Must find it."

His eyes rolled back in his head and he passed out. Well fuck.

I stood and hit her with power again. Siding and broken furniture crunched under my feet as I stepped inside the house. Minka lay in a prone heap on the floor, finally unconscious.

I picked up my phone and texted Ethan.

Got your problem. Want to take her off my hands?

She'd always needed her hands and her mouth to cast a spell. I rummaged through drawers and cabinets until I found something I could tie her up with. She lay on her stomach, so I gathered her hands behind her back and tied her as best I could. Frowning at the poor tie job, I went back to the kitchen and dug until I found duct tape. On my way back to her, I spotted a dirty washcloth and grabbed that, too.

Every witch worth her salt had duct tape handy. Once I had her trussed up like a roasting pig and knew she'd never be able to free herself, I flipped her over and shoved the dirty cloth in her mouth, sealing the cloth in with the gray tape. To keep it secure, I wrapped it around her head several times, catching the bulk of her hair inside.

Petty? Yes.

Worth the karma strike? Absolutely. She'd have a bitch of a time salvaging her hair. If she lived long enough to try.

Where are you? Ethan responded.

I dropped him a pin.

He was there in seconds, the only hint of surprise on his handsome face the slight lift of his eyebrows when he saw the destruction.

When he spotted Minka, his lips went thin. "This is her?"

I nodded. "She was never there for Soren."

"What about the other witches?"

"Still on the game board."

He bent down to peer at her. "That tape is going to be a bitch to get off." He glanced up at me. "Never seen you make a mistake like that."

I smiled. "No mistakes were made today."

He snorted and held up another potion. "What about this?"

"Pour it on her," I said. "She has enough magic to ensure it still works." There was no way I was freeing her hands or her mouth.

"Be careful not to loosen her mouth or her hands. Consider her extremely dangerous."

"What about eating?"

"I assume you know what you'll do with her within a few hours, yes?"

Ethan watched me. "I don't have to take her, you know. I can leave her here and come back later. If there's something you wish to do."

He spoke of killing her, something I'd thought about every single day for years. Instead, I allowed someone else to do the job for me, and look what happened. I might have killed Evie's dad.

Best friend of the year, I was not.

Ethan's brow furrowed. "Are you alright? You seem…off."

Cernunnos's power still buzzed in my veins and was making me feel like I'd downed ten espressos and topped it off with some crystal meth. I was doing my best to suppress most of the power because of the wonderful side effect of this particular gift of mine. One I did *not* want Ethan to experience. But yes, I was totally fine. I gave what I hoped was a reassuring smile.

Ethan sighed and shook his head. "Moira, I can't starve her to death."

"I mean, you *can*," I said hopefully.

He nudged Minka's body with his boot. "Have you called Soren?"

"Not yet."

"Does he know who she is?"

"No. I have no plans to inform him. As far as he's concerned, she's one of the witches trying to kill him."

Technically true. Soren didn't need to know he was a side quest while she drained everyone of their life force and magic.

"Turn her over to Soren. Or better yet, Evie." As much as I wanted my mother dead, I wanted her to suffer more. Evie didn't know what my mother had done to me. The moment I told her, Minka would know no end to her suffering.

I stared at my mother's still figure. "Do you have a lead-lined cell?"

Ethan grimaced. "You think she's that powerful?"

"I know she is." He hadn't asked about Cernunnos. The magic was so heavy in here, he wouldn't be able to detect his presence, either. Better for both of us.

"We have one on Keep grounds," Ethan admitted. "All Shifter Lords do."

I blinked in surprise. "Seriously?"

"We have hosts of mages who work for us. Occasionally, one will experience magic burn. Stick them in there for twenty-four hours and they come out good as new."

Magic burn was when a mage cycled through power too quickly and either collapsed in exhaustion or morphed into something wholly different from before. Lead suppressed magic. A witch or a mage locked inside wouldn't be able to perform a single spell, giving rest to one who burned out or suppressing one who could kill you with a twist of her fingers.

Like the woman lying at our feet.

"I suggest you stick her in there. Make sure she's out cold when you remove the restraints and have mages with you when you do."

"Moira—"

"I don't want anything to do with her. In fact, I'd rather never see her again for as long as I live." Maybe she'd rot in that cell.

I wondered again if I should kill her. My brain was screaming yes, and my cursed heart was whispering, she's still your mother…

Yes, well, she was also the kind of mother who abused and starved children. So shut up, brain.

Ethan rose and unscrewed the top on the potion. "Very well." He poured the potion all over Minka.

"I'll see you soon."

His words sounded like a warning.

Ethan crouched to touch my mother. A moment later they were gone.

I spun on my feet and hauled ass outside. Cernunnos was still splayed out on the ground.

I crouched beside him, relieved to see his eyes open. "Gods. Are you alright?"

"I'll be fine."

"You sure as shit don't look like you're fine."

Cernunnos lifted a bloody hand. I gripped it and helped him sit.

Animals poured from the trees and brush, encircling us as they watched warily.

"How could she have injured you so badly?"

"The bitch took me by surprise," he growled. "She possesses a fae weapon."

I went still. "I didn't see anything."

"She doesn't know it would harm you. Why would she tip her hand?"

I pretended I had no idea what he was talking about. "Excuse me?"

Cernunnos let out a heavy breath. "We'll talk later. Help me up so I can get us out of here. Then we'll purge the rest of my magic from your body before you combust, alright?"

I needed to stop hanging out with Evie's dad. He knew far too much about me for comfort.

CHAPTER
Twenty~One

We stayed in the ruins of Minka's home for over an hour. Surprisingly, one couch had survived the chaos, and I helped Cernunnos over, picking his legs up so he could settle on the cushions. I took that time to go through every inch of Minka's house.

She'd left her Book of Shadows behind. I picked it up, hissing at the oily feel of her magic clinging to the leather cover and parchment inside. Minka was going to be so pissed when she woke up and realized it was gone.

I didn't dare flip through the pages right now. Instead, I tucked the book into my bag and kept digging to see what else I could find. She had a cabinet full of difficult to source ingredients I happily plundered, and a notebook filled with her spidery scrawl.

I took that, too.

I also plucked a hairbrush from her bathroom sink—the better to spell her with if she somehow managed to get out of that cell Ethan planned to throw her in—and brand new bottles of very expensive shampoo and conditioner I confirmed were only that. No funny business on any of her bathroom products. Somehow that made her feel a little more human.

Which made me feel a little less.

Anyhow. Waste not. Want not.

The rest of the house looked as normal as a dark witch's home could be, or so I assumed, as I was not a dark witch and didn't hang around with anyone who was. I'd always disliked witches, though I put on a good front when I was in Joy Springs.

Once I finished my search, I came back into the living room to see Cernunnos sitting up.

"You look a little better."

"Are you ready?" He held out his hand.

"I am."

Once he was standing, I braced his big body against my hip. Cernunnos was warm, heavy, and very male. This might be sexy if he wasn't bleeding all over me.

"We can wait a little longer if we need to," I assured him.

"No," he growled. "Your mother isn't done with her carnage. We need to track down the weapon's maker and find out what it does and why she has it."

"Back to my apartment?"

Cernunnos shook his head. "I need to return to my land to finish healing. Will you come?"

He speared me with that ancient, swirling gaze. My mouth went dry.

"Um. I guess?"

He rolled his eyes. "You can't return to Rowan's lands brimming with my magic. You're bound to blow the place up."

"Fine." I slapped my hand in his. "I know how to purge this. I'm just not in a spot where I can safely do so."

He gave me an odd look. "Whyever not? There hasn't been a hint of the police since we arrived, which tells me either everyone hated Minka, or she has this place glamoured and under a sound ward. This is the perfect opportunity to let go."

I swallowed hard and shook my head. "There are mitigating factors."

Cernunnos frowned but shook his head. "We'll talk when we're back on my lands."

A moment later, we wobbled out of existence, Cernunnos's hold on his power tenuous enough to make me nervous.

WE STOOD in the god's living room. Without saying a word, Cernunnos went straight to the kitchen, dug a knife out of a drawer, and cut the rest of his shirt away.

I sucked in a breath at the massive, jagged slice bisecting his abdomen.

He grunted in pain as he sat down on a stool and examined the wound. "Moira. Come here."

I grimaced but walked toward him, a sick feeling in my gut at what he might ask me to do.

He flipped the knife over and held out the end. "Take it."

I hesitated. "This feels like it's about to turn into some Wild West field doctor shit."

Cernunnos was not amused. "The material is resistant to my magic."

"You can't push it out by yourself?"

"Correct."

I stared down at the knife. "So you want me to dig it out."

"Also correct."

"Are we close enough for me to dig shit out of your skin with a knife? Shouldn't this be something Evie does?"

He exhaled. "Is Evie here right now?"

"I feel like this is going to change our relationship forever."

"Moira. Can you please shut up and help?"

Ah shit. I did not want to do this. "Fine." I crouched down and took a look at the wound. "Whatever it is seems like it's stuck deep inside."

I rose. "Better if you're lying flat. Let's go to the couch."

And that is how the former fae king and I bonded.

But it took a lot of teeth gritting and name calling first.

Cernunnos was kind of a baby without his magic. The thought made me grin.

Once I'd managed to get every single iron shard out of his wound, the jagged edges began to close up almost immediately.

Cernunnos let out a small sigh. "Thank you."

I handed the knife back. "Let's maybe not tell Evie about this."

"Deal."

After a quick wash up, I made tea and brought a mug over to him. "This weapon's maker. Any idea who she is?"

"Weapons are common. Those able to take someone of my caliber are not. There are only two makers I know of capable of creating something like this. The more concerning question is how your mother was able to acquire one."

He frowned. "Speaking of. Is your mother still alive?"

I told him where she was. Cernunnos gave me a long look, and I squirmed at the disappointment in his swirling eyes.

"She's my mother," I said quietly.

He sipped his tea. "I wondered for a time whether Evie would try to kill Cliona."

"Totally different scenario. My mother is 100% guilty."

"Still. She perceived Cliona's actions to be unforgivable. Evie has always reacted vehemently when someone threatens the people she loves. What your mother did to you is arguably far worse, and yet, you stayed your hand, even when her death was almost assured."

I made the wrong decision. We both knew it.

"Thank you for trying."

Cernunnos shrugged. "Without that weapon, your mother would be dead." He paused and sipped his tea. "How does that make you feel?"

"I feel nothing," I answered honestly. "The world would be a better place if she was not in it. But to kill her myself..." My voice trailed off. "I'm not sure I could."

"There is a strong bond between a mother and daughter, no matter how bad the relationship is. Part of that societal, part is ingrained in our DNA. Even I would hesitate to strike a blow against family."

He wasn't blaming me, but I could hear the disappointment in his voice. "Do you trust the Shifter Lord to keep her secure?"

"As much as I trust anyone," I admitted. "He has a lead-lined cell, and I've ensured he knows how dangerous he is."

"He's an arrogant male."

I snorted. "And you are not?"

Cernunnos flashed a smile. "Perhaps so, but after having iron shards dug from my skin, I will temper my arrogance next time."

I changed the subject. "You know where these weapons makers are."

He inclined his head. "One lives in Emberwood. You might know her."

When he spoke the name, my hand jerked, sloshing tea over the edge.

"Are you serious?"

"The Maker has asked for privacy and takes no commissions. She is all but retired and wishes to put those days behind her."

"Shit," I muttered. Evie wanted the same thing and ended up being dragged kicking and screaming back into a world she wanted no part of. I hoped I wasn't about to do the same to someone else.

"As soon as you're ready to take me back, I'll speak with her."

"Eat with me first," Cernunnos said. "I'll take you home right afterward."

When I nodded, he smiled. "And do not think I've forgotten about your vampiric gift, Moira. We will speak of it later."

Of course he hadn't. Dude had a mind like a steel trap.

Twenty~Two

I hovered outside the entrance to Metal & Mayhem, wondering how best to approach her. I thought Ari and I were well on our way to building a friendship, but this would throw it right off the rails.

Now that I knew who she really was, her occupation choice made a whole lot more sense. She was Emberwood's premier jewelry artist; her pieces were shown in galleries all over the state. I knew she'd been approached to explore featuring work across the country, but she'd declined.

If you wanted to stay under the radar, I guess working in a small town would do it. Unfortunately for her, Ari was way too talented not to blow up. The perils of genius, I guess.

I inhaled and pushed the boutique door open. The familiar smell of bergamot and rose teased my senses. She had a diffuser going somewhere that pumped the scent through the store. When I asked about it once, she'd given me a small bottle, and told me it relaxed customers. Then she grinned conspiratorially.

"The more relaxed they are, the more they buy."

Not that she ever had trouble selling anything she made. Ari was hella talented.

I liked Ari. A lot. The thought of her giving Mom something designed to kill a god didn't sit right with me.

The woman in question was working with a customer when I walked in. When she spotted me, her face lit up in a smile and she waved.

I waved back, but something on my face made her smile falter. Her brow furrowed and she held a finger up. I busied myself with perusing her new stock.

Ari worked in metals. Silver, brass, bronze, gold, titanium—any type of metal you wanted, she sourced it. She focused on sculptural jewelry, things you won't find elsewhere. I owned several pairs of her earrings, most in mixed metals.

She had a back area where she sold gemstone jewelry, none of which I could afford. Or I could afford it if I became a one-meal-a-day faster for a month or so.

The woman Ari was helping paid for her purchase and hurried out.

Ari's face was wary. "Is this a conversation we should take to the back?"

"I'm afraid so."

She nodded, a haunted look appearing in her silvery-gray eyes. "Alright then. Give me a moment."

Ari locked the shop door and pulled the shades. "Come on then."

We walked past the gemstone area and back into a comfortable and tastefully decorated office.

Ari motioned me inside and shut the door with a wave of her hand. "Please, sit." She let out a heavy sigh. "I'm afraid I know why you're here."

Ari, like most fae, had an ethereal look to her. Evie was one of the few exceptions to this rule. My best friend was a stunner, but her beauty held an earthier, more human look, and after everything, I wondered if that had less to do with her fae heritage and more to do with her connection to the world. Evie seemed more tethered here than anywhere else.

Ari stood out among even the fae. She was tall and willowy, with dark hair and light eyes. Her face was heart-shaped with the tiniest dent in her chin. High cheekbones dusted with a shimmer of color lent her a slightly feline look. The woman was stunning, but she was humble.

And from the way she slumped into her chair and sighed, the woman was tired too.

"Which weapon?"

Ah. So she did know.

I dug into my purse and pulled out a small velvet bag and tossed it to her. She caught it and dumped the contents onto her desk.

Ari stared at the iron shards, some still flecked with Cernunnos's blood. Magic the smell of iron and copper rose in the air. Her eyes went molten silver. As I watched, the shards began to wiggle as if Ari shook the table underneath. The blood dried and flaked, falling away from the metal.

"This weapon struck someone extremely powerful." Ari's voice sounded deep and otherworldly. "Who possesses the Star of Scathach?"

She waved her hand, and the shards fell to the table. Her power died, and when she looked at me once more, her eyes were back to their normal silvery shade.

"I was hoping you could tell me who should have the weapon."

Ari rubbed her hand over her face. "Scathach. If the weapon is not in her possession, the warrior must be dead."

Grief flickered over her face. "You know who has it, don't you?"

I nodded. "My mother."

Ari frowned. "Why would your mother be in possession of a god killer?"

She blinked, her attention going to the blood on the table. "Oh gods. Does this belong to Cernunnos?"

I smiled faintly.

Ari paled. "Is he on his way here?"

"He's been surprisingly chill about almost dying in a witch's backyard, so I don't think so."

The fae slumped and let out a slow breath. "I've just come to this place and…I like it here. I would stay if I could."

The haunted look on her face struck a chord. I knew what it was like to have to run all the time. "He will not be the one to force you to leave. I promise."

Actually, I had no idea, but it was a good sign he hadn't come with me.

"Can you tell me what the weapon does? Besides the obvious one?"

Ari nodded. "I made the Star for the warrior millennia ago so she could retire in peace. Some of the gods were angry that she refused to keep training our young warriors, but Scathach was tired and only sought respite."

She frowned at the shards. "The weapon is damaged. I do not know if the functionality will be the same. Our weapons are not fragile, but striking someone like Cernunnos with one is ill-advised unless you're in a life-or-death situation."

I grimaced. "To be fair, she was."

Her eyebrows flicked up in curiosity. "How does Cernunnos fare?"

"I had to dig iron shards from his skin, which made him grumpy, but he seemed whole and hardy afterward."

Ari closed her eyes in relief. "Good. I would hate to cause Evie pain. Does she know?"

"No." I leaned forward. "And we are not going to tell her. Cool?"

Ari blinked. "Err. Of course. But if she asks me directly, I will not lie."

"Doubtful Evie will find out you're some legendary fae weapon's maker and come at you with a *Hey, did your weird Star weapon almost kill my dad?*, but if she does, I'll give you that one."

"Fair." She reached under the desk and came up with a large

purse. "We must find the weapon and properly store it or return it to Scathach if she still lives."

I stared at her. "Um. We?"

Ari's sharp nod made me nervous. "Yes. We. I am its maker. A fae weapon will never resist its maker's call. If I'm close enough, I can retrieve it."

My phone buzzed. "Fine, but only if you're cool with hanging around Lords and gods. They seem to be all up my butt these days."

A ghost of a smile flickered over her mouth. "I am well acquainted with the gods, Moira. Though I wish to be in peace, a damaged fae weapon in the wrong hands cannot be ignored."

My phone buzzed again as Ari rose from her chair.

"Come, gods touched. Let us go."

I froze for a second. Ari had never referred to me as such. Only Cernunnos. The fae must see something around me others didn't. One more thing to worry about. I put that one firmly in the *investigate later* category.

"Don't you need to keep the shop open?" I worried when I shut my tea shop down during the day and couldn't imagine how much money Ari might lose if she closed early.

She shook her head. "The residents here are used to my temperamental ways. I am an artist and shut the shop down when whimsy or creativity take me. No one will question me."

My phone buzzed one more time.

"Do you need to get that?" Ari asked.

I pulled my cell out. Soren.

Call me.

CALL.

CALL NOW!

I swore under my breath and called. He answered on the first ring.

"There's something wrong with my wolves. Everyone is sick." The panic in his voice was evident.

"And you?"

"Fucking fine," he growled. "Has to be the witches. Can you get here soon?"

"Not sure how I can help with food poisoning—"

"Moira, godsdammit can you just—"

"I can get us there," Ari said quietly.

I added supernatural hearing to her powers list.

"I'll be there in a minute."

Soren hung up without another word.

Ari watched me. "Want to fill me in?"

"Not really."

She chuckled. "Witches and poisoning?"

"Soren put his dick in multiple places he shouldn't and pissed off a dangerous coven. They hired my mother to help them, and of course, she had an ulterior motive."

"To find you?" Ari tilted her head. "You do have the sense of someone hiding in plain sight."

I said nothing.

"Moira." Her voice turned contemplative. "You and I are the only ones in this shop. I thought we were coming to form a friendship. Is this not the case?"

Dammit. It was the case. "You don't bare your soul to new friends. They'll run away screaming."

Ari grinned. "No need for soul baring," she promised. "But a little bit of honesty is always a good start." She held open the door. "Let's see. You know I'm a fae weapons maker."

"Noooo…" I drawled. "I know you're one of two fae weapons makers who can create things that kill freaking gods."

Ari sighed. "Alright. Let's meet in the middle then. We don't have to bare our souls, but we should share one hard fact about ourselves."

"No fair. I already know yours, so you don't have to do anything."

Ari crossed her arms over her chest. "Fine. My father is a god. He's a real dick, and I hate him."

I had a feeling she wasn't one of the lesser fae. "Please tell me it's not Cernunnos."

Ari laughed, her eyes sparkling. "No. Evie is not my sister. His name is Goibnui. My gift comes from him."

"And your mom?"

She shrugged. "No idea. All I know is she's fae."

"Are you hiding from him?"

She grimaced. "Not quite. We exist in an uneasy peace. He, and I suppose Cernunnos now, are the only ones who know where I am."

I gestured to her jewelry. "You've grown too popular. Won't be long before others figure it out."

"I don't do interviews and I have an anti-tech charm installed in the shop."

"I just got three texts." I held up my hand. "Anyway, we have to go. Soren is freaking out."

Ari held out her hand. "With Cernunnos around, I'm sure you know the drill."

As soon as our fingers interlaced, Ari's cold magic swept over my skin and we were gone.

We appeared inside Soren's Keep, which told me he'd either dropped his wards, or the witches had dropped them for him. The Lord sat on the front steps of his porch with his head in his hands. He was still alive and apparently uninjured.

"Is that the guy with the magic dick?" Ari whispered.

Soren's head jerked up.

"Yep. If you haven't noticed, Lords tend to have sharper hearing than normal shifters."

"Huh," Ari said. "Good to know."

He stared at Ari, a thin ring of gold around his irises. "Moira? Who is this?" His voice held a slight growl. He wasn't angry. Not exactly. But he sounded weird.

Ari didn't give me the chance to answer. "My name is Ari Tavish. Moira needed a lift, and I was happy to oblige."

The sound of retching came from somewhere to the left. "Everyone's hurling," Soren said miserably. "I have no idea what to do."

Ari gave him a weird look. "Shifters don't get sick. They're either under the influence of a spell or they've been poisoned."

Soren gave her a dark look. "I'm aware."

Ari clicked her tongue. "Then why are you sitting on your ass doing nothing?"

Soren rose. His eyes turned full golden.

"Uh. Ari?"

She scoffed. "I am not afraid of a Lord, Moira."

"You should be, fae." Soren stalked toward her.

Ari rolled her eyes. "Come, wolf. Take me to your people. I will try to identify what the witches used."

Soren's steps hitched. "Witch. You don't order me around."

"Fine. I'll see to them myself." Ari stalked away.

I pressed my lips together to hide my smile.

Soren blinked a few times before he looked at me. "Is she always like this?"

I shrugged. "No idea. I just buy my jewelry from her." A little untrue. The first time seeing Ari in the wild was just as surprising for me as it was for Soren.

The Lord sighed and took off after her.

I stared at their backs and shook my head. Hopefully Soren wouldn't try to sleep with her, too. She might magic his balls right off.

I followed after them, keeping my eyes peeled for any witches. With the wards down, anything could happen.

At least ten shifters were lying on the ground, curled into the fetal position, groaning in agony.

I gagged when I got too close, the smell of vomit overwhelming. Ari crouched beside one of the shifters, her hands on his pale face. Her eyes glowed molten silver, and her lips were slightly parted.

Soren crouched beside her, a furrow on his brow as he watched her. The poor bastard wasn't quite sure how to take Ari. No Lord knew how to take a woman who was unafraid of them.

But they were all having to live in a brand new world now that Evie had opened the doors. She wasn't afraid of any of them. In fact, they were all a little afraid of her. I had a feeling Ari, if she ever stepped into society, might be worse than Evie.

She lifted her hands, her eyes returning to normal. "Did they all eat the same thing?"

"Catered food," Soren said.

Ari and I exchanged a glance. "The witches intercepted the food. Maybe paid someone off to give them access."

The healing power living inside me wasn't rising up. No one here was close to death. I'm sure the shifters disagreed, but Fee's power only rose when someone was either in grave danger or had been seriously wounded.

Food poisoning didn't count, it seemed.

I pulled out my cell and texted Ben, one of the other Lords. "Soren, are you cool allowing Ben in to take a look?"

He was a big burly Lord and had acted as Caelan's Healer once upon a time. Now he was a Lord and managed territory around the Midwest. On a side note, he and Evie had danced around each other for a while, and the idiot probably could have married her if he got his head out of his ass. Spoiler: he did not, in fact, pull his head out of his ass, and Rowan won the day.

I liked Ben. He was a little set in his ways, but healers, as a general rule, tended to be good people.

Myself excluded. My healing gift was not inherent or even wanted.

"The wards are down," Soren said with a grunt. "Any damn body could waltz in here right now. Might as well be someone who can help."

Alrighty then. Soren was grumpy.

I fired off another text to Ben and then one to Evie's dad to see if he'd transport the Lord if he had time to pop by. He wouldn't appreciate being used as a taxi service, but this wasn't a normal circumstance.

"How many others are there?"

"Everyone but me is affected," Soren said.

I went still as his words finally penetrated. If every shifter was down, this would be the perfect opportunity to strike.

"Shit," I muttered. "Ari, be ready."

The fae stood up and dusted her pants off. "Three against a coven?" She winced. "Poor odds."

Ari slid a look over to Soren. "Maybe two against a coven. Soren seems to be a little useless right now."

"Watch it, witch," Soren growled, still staring down at his ill shifters.

Ari sighed. "I am no witch, wolf. You'd do well to watch your tongue around me."

A shift in the wind and Cernunnos stood there with a disgruntled Lord.

"Ben," I said in relief. "Thanks so much for coming."

He gave my father a dark look. "Didn't have much choice," he said with a rumble. "Less than a minute after I got your text, Cernunnos stood in my office." He spread his hands out. "And here we are."

"I let you take your bag," Cernunnos said mildly.

Ben rolled his eyes. A second later, he spotted Ari. Tension pulled in the air between them. Ari's eyes narrowed.

"You are more than you seem, Healer."

Ben grunted. "You're one to talk."

My gaze bounced between them. "Uh. Ari, this is Ben, the Shifter Lord of the Midwest. Ben, this is Ari."

One of his eyebrows rose. "Just Ari?"

"She owns a jewelry store in Emberwood," I supplied. Ari probably had an annoyingly long, fancy title, but I didn't know it, nor had she shared.

They were still staring at each other. And not in a good way. Both of them looked like they wanted to go for the other's throats.

"Well," I said slowly, "we think witches intercepted a catered meal. No idea if it's a spell or simply spoiled food. Soren is the only one who didn't eat the food."

Ben snorted. "Not enough caviar to suit your fancy tastes, Lord?"

Soren's lips thinned. "Don't start with me. Can you help or not?"

A flash of teeth was Ben's answer before he walked over, keeping a wide berth around Ari. He knelt beside a shifter and touched two fingers to their throat. Magic rose in the air, gentle and cool. Ben's magic always reminded me of a calm sea. His eyes turned an electric shade of blue.

Ari came to stand beside me. "How well do you know him?"

"Not too well. He's like a side character in our main quest."

Ari gave me the side eye. "I want to understand that, but I'm not there yet."

"I like Ben, but he's grumpy."

"I heard that," Ben growled.

"It's true," I said hotly.

Ari kept staring at Ben. "He looks familiar."

"He hasn't been a Lord long. Maybe you met before then."

Ari's lips pursed. Maybe.

Ben checked each shifter before rising. "They're under the influence of a spell. No one is in any real danger of anything other than shitting themselves for the next few hours."

Soren grimaced. Ben speared him with a furious look. "To my knowledge, this is mostly your doing. I can help speed their healing along, but the spell isn't designed to last long."

Ari stilled. "Moira. Something is coming."

Ben's smile didn't reach his eyes. "It seems the witches felt taking on a Keep, even one as small as yours would test even their mettle. You're lucky your shifters aren't dead. Next time, be smarter than this."

Soren's eyes began to glow.

"Keeping your dick in your pants won't hurt either."

Ari snorted.

Soren lunged for Ben. A tendril of emerald and silver magic flashed, freezing the angry Lord in place. "Your battle is not with him," Cernunnos said. "Turn and see what you have reaped."

A massive cloud of darkness rolled toward Soren's Keep.

Soren swore, a rare look of desperation on his face.

"Can you throw the wards up?" I asked.

Cernunnos thought about it for a moment. "I could, I suppose. The more important question is why they're down in the first place."

Soren blanched. "I had to let the caterers in."

Ari covered her mouth to stop her laughter, but she wasn't all that successful.

"Why didn't you put them back up?" I stared at Soren like he was the biggest idiot on the planet.

"When I tried, I couldn't!" His face took on a look of raw panic.

Cernunnos frowned. His eyes began to swirl, and I assumed he was looking at the wards. A moment later, he slowly nodded. "Your wards are gone, Lord. Destroyed. If I were you, I'd make that first on the list and push chasing after paramours down to perhaps number four or five."

"Cernunnos," I warned.

We eyed the coming storm. My phone buzzed.

What the hell is going on over there? So much magic is buzzing against my senses, I can't nap!

I stared at the message. Evie never napped. Was this code for I can't indulge in a little mid-afternoon delight?

My response was quick and to the point. *Soren pissed off the witches and took advantage of his idiocy.*

Ah. Sounds like things are totally normal then.

We got it under control. Don't worry.

Evie sent me an eyeroll emoji back.

Oh yeah. She was definitely going to worry.

"Any idea what's coming toward us?" Ben asked.

To his credit, he sounded unrattled about the fast approaching cloud of blackness.

Cernunnos focused. "I'm not as familiar with witch magic, but that seems like a death curse. You might want to do something."

Another shift of wind and my best friend appeared in the clearing. She looked at all of us, frowned when she spotted Ari and gave me a questioning look, then turned to see the massive cloud approaching us.

"What the fuck!"

I barked a laugh. Evie put her hands on her hips. "Dad! What the hell. Why are the wards down? Why are you standing there doing absolutely nothing?" She spun. "And why the hell is Ben here?"

Her sharp gaze spotted the groaning shifters. "And why the hell does it smell like vomit?"

She blew out a heavy breath. "You know. I do one favor for you, Soren, and things get shot to hell!" Evie pointed at the cloud. "I can only assume that thing is coming for you?"

Soren's defeated look only seemed to piss Evie off even more. "Where the hell is the arrogant, know-it-all Lord who's annoyed me for over a year now? Why are you standing there with your index finger up to its knuckle inside your nose?"

"Evie," Cernunnos said quietly.

"And why the hell is the Emberwood jeweler here!" Her eyes began to blaze with color.

"Evie," her dad said once more.

She spun on her heel. "WHAT!"

"This isn't on you to solve."

"It's on my land! Soren is merely borrowing said land, and I swear to the gods if this is some plague meant to kill everything it touches, I'm going to murder Soren if this shit doesn't do it first, then I'm never ever going to grant another favor to the godforsaken Lords for as long as I live!"

I covered my mouth to hide my smile. Gods how I loved her.

"I'm here because something I created got into the wrong hands," Ari said, watching my friend with a newfound respect.

Evie's brow furrowed. "Like a necklace or something?"

"Or something," I said, so Ari didn't feel like she had to reveal any more than she wanted to. "We can discuss it later."

Ben and Soren both eyed Ari with curiosity.

Evie swiped a hand down. "Regardless. What are we doing to stop this right now?"

Cernunnos shrugged. "I wasn't going to do a thing."

"Dad!" Evie snapped. "What the hell?"

"I'm not supposed to get involved," he said, but there was a twinkle in his eye. The asshole was enjoying himself.

"You get involved in everything all the time!" Evie's eyes were blazing with color now. "From what I understand, you've been all up Moira's ass for the past few days."

She looked at me. "I have no idea what's going on there, but I swear if you two are sleeping together, I never, ever, ever want to know about it."

I almost laughed, but Evie was serious. "We are not sleeping together."

Her eyes narrowed. "I don't like that I can't tell if you're lying to me."

Ben started laughing. "She smells like him, Evie. Only due to proximity. I scent nothing amiss."

I threw my hands up. "Alright. Stop fucking sniffing me, please! It's super creepy when you do that."

Evie closed her eyes and exhaled. "Fine. I'm not saying no. You're both adults, but Moira, please only sleep with my dad if you're sure you want to like..." Her voice trailed off. "Get married or something."

She rubbed the spot between her brows. "But I will never call you Mom. That's weird enough to make my head explode."

I eyed her. "Are you alright?" She was rarely so emotional. I'd seen her get agitated, but today was something different.

"I'm fine," she snapped, which was also unlike her. "But for the love of the gods, will someone, anyone, please tell me what the hell that thing is moving toward us?"

"Death curse," Cernunnos said cheerfully.

Evie blanched. "Meant for Soren?"

"Yup." Dad grinned. "Turns out witches don't like being Eskimo sisters."

I blinked. "How the hell do you know what that means?"

"I learn a lot at that shifter bar downtown."

Evie looked positively scandalized. "Dad! I'm going to get you banned."

"You're the one who suggested I spend more time with 'normal' people."

Ari watched us like a ping-pong match, a look of delight on her face. "You think shifters are normal?"

Evie sighed the sigh of a woman who's had this argument a hundred times over. "They're more normal than that guy!" She pointed an accusing finger at her father.

The spell cloud barreled toward us.

I couldn't help with wards. Not my thing, and none of the weird magic I had would affect them for good or ill. Cernunnos seemed perfectly content to watch Soren die a horrible death, and Evie seemed stunned none of us were doing anything.

I was totally asking for a raise when I got home.

"Soren!"

He stared at the horizon with a resigned expression on his face. "Yes?"

"You altered the original wards. Why?"

He blinked in surprise. "Err. You can tell?"

Claws grew from Evie's fingers. Oh yeah. She was really annoyed now.

I leaned over and murmured in his ear. "I'd stop asking stupid questions and answer her questions."

"I wanted to know if you were outside the wards."

None of us missed the sullen tone.

A ring of crimson circled Evie's glowing azure and watermelon tourmaline eyes. "This is my land."

Soren cringed. "I'm aware."

She turned to look at the cloud. "Maybe I should let it come," she mused. "It'd serve your ass right."

Soren sucked in a breath. "Evie!"

She stood frozen, her eyes locked on the horizon. "You Lords are so used to me stepping in to save you."

Even Ben looked discomfited by that.

"But what have you done for me?"

Now I was really concerned. Evie never asked for anything, nor did she expect anything in return when she did something for someone else.

She wasn't wrong, but I'd never heard her speak like this.

"Evie?"

She blinked and looked at me. Her face softened. "I'm fine, Moira. I promise."

Evie reached out and took my hand. "Sometimes people need to learn their own lessons, don't you think?"

Before I could blink, Evie ripped me into the ether, away from Soren and the black cloud of death coming his way.

Twenty-Four

I sucked in a gasping breath and slumped over onto the grass in Rowan's front yard. Evie's way of travel was not as smooth as Cernunnos's. Hers felt like someone had sucked out my soul with a Wet Vac.

She knelt beside me, her cool fingertips brushing my forehead. "Sorry," she murmured. A touch of her magic swirled into my skin, relieving the nausea and vertigo the travel caused. "Still getting used to taking people with me."

Cernunnos appeared a few seconds later, hauling Ari and Ben with him. He was chuckling to himself when he spotted Evie.

"About time," he murmured, approval brimming in his voice.

Evie was still annoyed with him. "I didn't do it for you."

"I'd rather you do it for you," he said.

Ari spoke up. "You're just going to leave him to it?"

I sent a message to Ethan skimming over the sordid details of what just happened.

Evie rolled her eyes. "Of course I won't. Provided Soren gets his people inside the main Keep house, he should be safe. I have the ability to ward anywhere I wish. I figure he has about five minutes to get his people to safety. I'll snap the ward over the house, and the spell should roll harmlessly over the top."

I sank against Evie's dad. "Thank fuck."

Evie laughed. "I'm not a total monster."

Ari was staring at Evie like she'd grown horns. "And if he doesn't get them inside?"

"I can only do so much," Evie responded. "I'm tired of Soren's shit. If he isn't smart and motivated enough to at least try to get himself and his people out of harm's way, then maybe he deserves to die."

Ben started to laugh, the sound a deep rumble within his chest. He wiped a hand over his face. "Things have been quiet for so long I'd forgotten what it was like to work with you all."

Ari's face was pale, and her eyes were wide. "You guys are ruthless."

"You would be too if you had to work with the Lords all the time," Evie said dryly.

Rowan came outside. He was handsome—all the Lords were, but I found Rowan to be stunning. Mostly because of how much he loved Evie. He was shorter than Soren, but still taller than Evie. Devilish hazel eyes that brimmed with warmth every time he looked at his wife widened slightly when he spotted all of us.

His lips twitched when he spotted Ben and Ari. "Dare I ask what happened?"

"Evie scared the shit out of Soren," I said cheerily.

"He thinks he's about to die," added Ben.

Ari said nothing.

"He's not going to die," Evie said with exasperation.

"If he figures out what he needs to do," Ari added, then let out a hysterical giggle.

Evie shrugged. "Pretty much."

Rowan gently dragged Evie against his chest and kissed the top of her head. His hands wrapped around her waist. "Think he'll figure it out?"

"Fifty-fifty," I said.

Rowan only nodded. I loved that about the guy. Not much riled him up. When it came to Evie, he supported every decision she made, even when it was insane. He'd question her if he thought she might be going the wrong way, but ultimately, he left things up to her.

I'd give my left tit for a guy like that.

"Did you tell Ethan?"

My phone rang.

I winced.

"You texted him?" Rowan asked, his eyes dancing with mirth.

"If I make him mad enough, he'll blow through the stash of travel potions I left."

Evie grinned. "And then he can't pop in and blow up at you in person."

I pointed finger guns at her. "Exactamundo."

A pop of air revealed Ethan, chest heaving with fury.

"Are you KIDDING me?" he roared.

I crossed my arms over my chest. "Are you aware you wasted a potion to yell at me for leaving Soren to die when you could have used one to go help him?"

He blinked. His eyes widened in horror. Rowan and Ben were obviously losing the battle not to laugh their asses off.

Evie opened her mouth, probably to tell him she had it under control, but at the almost imperceptible shake of my head, she pressed her lips together and looked at the ground.

He patted his chest pocket, swore viciously under his breath, then patted his pants pocket to reveal another potion. His teeth tore the lid off and he downed the other one.

"This is NOT over!" he yelled just before he disappeared.

Ben let out a hoot of laughter.

"How many does he have left?" Evie asked.

I tilted my head and squinted at the sky as I counted backward. "Four, I think. He only brought two with him today, so I have some time before he finds his way back here."

"You sure you want to keep pissing Ethan off?" Rowan asked, amusement in his eyes.

I lifted a shoulder in a careless shrug. "It's fun to rattle him. He'll be alright."

Ari slowly shook her head. "You are all insane."

"Yeah," I said with a heavy exhale. "I guess I should have warned you."

Her eyes warmed. "No. It's wonderful. I'm just taken by surprise, that's all. It's been a while since I've seen such a close-knit clan."

I eyed Ben. "Not all of us are. But we all know each other, and everyone is used to Evie's shenanigans."

Evie let out an affronted noise. "Shenanigans you were involved in, too!"

"Yes, well, you went and got married, so now you should be shenanigan free."

Rowan barked a laugh at that one. "I can assure you, she is far from that."

"Ari, once Ethan cools down, I'll take you to see my mother. If she has what you're seeking, you should know, right?"

Ari nodded. "Yes. The item will call to me."

"I'll wait a day or so before contacting him. Mom's in a lead-lined cell, so she shouldn't be going anywhere any time soon."

Evie's brows went up, but she didn't prod. I loved that about her, too, even as guilt hit me. She deserved to know about my childhood, the things I'd done to survive, and yet, I kept shutting her out.

I promised myself I'd talk to her. Soon.

Ari touched her hand to her heart, nodded to everyone, and disappeared in a swirl of silver.

"May I ask why you're hanging out with the town jeweler?" Rowan said in his patient drawl.

I wouldn't say anything with Ben here. "I was at her shop when Soren called. She offered to drop everything and haul me over there."

"Ah. Lucky she was there," was all Rowan said, though I knew he'd be asking more questions later.

"Very," I agreed.

"Ben, are you ready to go home?" Cernunnos rolled his eyes at me when I glanced his way. "One more taxi fare won't kill you," I said sweetly.

The large shifter grunted and stared up at the sky. "I got time for a beer if you do," he said to Rowan.

"Always time for a beer," he agreed. He jerked his head toward the main house, and Ben followed.

With me, Evie, and Cernunnos left, Evie sank to the ground and sighed. She stuck her fingers in the dirt. Magic rose around us, tingling against my skin. The smell of jasmine and honeysuckle filled the air, a scent I always identified with Evie's power.

Her eyes turned colorful, and flowers popped into existence in a circle around her. Alright. That one was new, too. Flowers weren't uncommon around here, but they normally didn't rise when she wasn't working powerful magic.

My eyes narrowed. Cernunnos shook his head once, seemingly warning me not to say anything.

When Evie's eyes cleared and she'd withdrawn her magic, she sighed and yawned. "The wards are up. I counted over a hundred bodies inside the Keep house."

"Looks like the idiot got his shit together." Relief filled me. While I didn't think Evie was wrong, I was surprised she'd let it go this far. Would she have let Soren die if he hadn't made the decision to get his people inside?

All signs pointed to yes.

That made something uncomfortable twist inside me. If Evie had been willing to let a Shifter Lord, someone she didn't hate, go to his death, why couldn't I kill someone who'd been unbearably cruel to me for my entire childhood? Was I that weak?

"Will you continue to allow him to share your land?" Cernunnos asked.

"I hate to kick him out. The poor bastard needed a break."

"There are no women over there," I said and laughed out loud when I thought how much Soren's poor peter must be suffering from the lack.

"There's an entire coven of witches if he's really willing to risk it all," Evie said with a grin.

I groaned. "Don't tempt him. He's just horny enough to try."

Cernunnos shook his head. "Penises have been responsible for most of this world's trouble since the dawn of time. You'd think they'd eventually realize it."

"Ha!" Evie crowed. "If anything, they've gotten worse!"

Couldn't disagree. We were a world ruled by sex in a way. Just look at the billions poured into the sex industry. The humans were just as bad, if not worse. "Sad state of affairs," I agreed. "One day I hope we'll see some women in power."

"Wouldn't that be something?" Evie mused.

"You are in power, dummy."

Evie zapped me with a vine she sent snapping out of the ground. "You're not allowed to call your queen a dummy."

"Yes, well, she is sometimes." We grinned at each other.

"I'd love to see a Shifter Lady in power." Evie sighed. "I would have suggested it if Soren crumbled into dust."

"I'd like to see it, too." I toyed with the soft grass. "Where's the spell at?"

Evie lay flat on her back. "Back to the witches. They'll try again. I'm sure of it."

I rolled over closer to her and took her hand. "Evie?"

She closed her eyes. "Hmmm?"

"Are you okay?"

A serene smile played upon her lips. "I'm perfect, Moira."

For once, I actually believed her.

Twenty~Five

Cernunnos was waiting for me on my porch when I made it home sometime after dark. Evie and Rowan offered to feed me, and I rarely passed up a meal with friends, so I stayed and hung out with them and Ben, who surprisingly agreed to stay too.

All I wanted was to faceplant in my bed, but Cernunnos wanted something.

I rummaged for my keys. "I'm tired."

Cernunnos's brows lifted. "I won't be long."

Once I unlocked the door, I waved him inside.

My shoes came off first, then I pulled my hair clip out, allowing the bulk to fall almost to my waist. Haircuts and maintenance had fallen by the wayside over the past year, and now I kinda liked it long. I shrugged off my pullover sweater and went straight to my room to pull on a pair of cotton modal pants and a soft cardigan.

When I came out, Cernunnos was pouring us both a cup of tea. He handed one to me without a word.

I went straight to the living room, curled in my recliner, and wound my blanket around me like a serpent.

Cernunnos perched on the edge of the couch. "Does anyone else know what you can do?"

So we were jumping right in with both feet, were we?

"I'm not sure. Do they?"

A flash of white teeth in the dim light was his only reaction. "Your secrets are always safe with me, gods touched."

"Mom's experimentation was thorough." As if being forced into vampirism wasn't bad enough, Mom decided she didn't want a child forever. Only it was too late to change the decision. Looking back, I wasn't exactly grateful for what she'd done, but if she hadn't, I would have been stuck in a child's body forever.

"And this was a side effect?"

I nodded.

"You can draw on anyone's power if you consume their blood." He sounded curious. That's all.

But my back was up. I'd never told a soul about this. There was no way he should have known what I could do.

"How did you know?"

"I didn't. Suspicion isn't knowing."

"I can't imagine you'd hand over your blood to just anyone." I might have saved our lives, but something about the incident didn't feel right. Blood meant power and control. Why had he trusted me with such a precious resource? I could use it to my advantage whenever I wanted.

He kicked off his shoes and lounged on my couch. I would never get used to having a god hanging around drinking my tea. "Do I need to worry?"

"You know the answer to that," I grumbled.

"Then I chose correctly."

I took a sip of my tea and glanced down at my cup. Damn. Cernunnos knew how to brew a fantastic cup of Earl Grey.

"Personal blend," he said when he noticed my attention. "I source it from a fae contact."

"I had no idea you drank Earl Grey."

"You introduced it to me. Someone like me can't exactly walk into a local shop without causing issues, so I had to find some-where else to buy it."

"Emberwood is used to you by now. Lots of people carry this."

"Few ever truly get used to me."

"I could have gotten it for you."

"Moira. We aren't talking about tea. We're talking about you."

I sank further into the couch cushions. "I'd rather talk about tea."

"I'm well aware," Cernunnos said dryly. "How long do you carry the power?"

I didn't want to answer the question because if I did, I'd reveal too much.

"Last time, I siphoned the rest of my power from you. If I hadn't, how long would you have hung on to it?"

"A while," I said.

Cernunnos scratched his chin. "A week?"

I didn't answer.

"Two?"

His eyebrows went up when I stayed silent. Cernunnos leaned forward, balancing the mug on his knee. "You are not saying you keep those powers, are you?"

I didn't keep them at the same level he could wield his or whoever's power I borrowed. But I did keep some. And that was why I'd never told a single soul.

No one else had these powers. If they did, they were doing the same thing I was.

Keeping their mouths shut.

Cernunnos let out a soft exhale. "Am I the only one who knows?"

I nodded.

"How often do you drink blood?"

"What kind of question is that?"

"Humor me." Cernunnos swung his legs onto the couch.

"Not often. Less often these days." Now that I was living on a shifter compound where the residents could smell every damned thing.

"Where do you source your blood?"

I squirmed uncomfortably. Unused to speaking so openly about this subject, I clamped my lips shut.

"Moira. It's you and me. No one else is here. I already know your secret. Allow me to help you."

"How would knowing where I source my blood help me?"

"You're sourcing from a human blood bank, aren't you?"

Human blood banks were safe. There was no chance of me slurping down some weird magic I had no idea how to control, and I didn't have to go hunting.

I nodded.

Cernunnos made a hmm noise. "Moira."

I curled my fingers around my mug. "It's late. I'm really tired. Can we talk about this tomorrow?"

His eyes swirled with annoyance. "You're a vampire and more. Don't you think it's odd how fatigued you are?"

I frowned at him. "No. I've been running nonstop."

Cernunnos rose. "I will sleep here tonight."

I opened my mouth to protest.

"Tomorrow, we will source you other blood." His face turned contemplative. "I purged my blood and power from your system without realizing exactly what you are and how it might affect you." He dipped his head. "My apologies."

I had no idea what he was talking about. "Why are you being weird?"

He held his hand out and helped me up, but this time he didn't let go. "Unless..."

Cernunnos drew me closer, his other hand sliding around my back.

"Umm."

"You've been tired for years, haven't you?" He released my fingers and slid his other hand through my hair, cradling the back of my head. "Eventually, you got used to the feeling of fatigue and compensated for it."

My heart began to pound.

"When you took my blood, sweet Moira, did the power sizzle through your veins? Did you feel invincible for a brief moment in time?"

It did. I had. My throat worked. He drew me closer, pressing our bodies together.

"Umm," I said again, because what else was there to say? His chest was rock hard with muscle and so warm I wanted to burrow into him like a cat.

"Shhh."

I was plastered against Evie's dad. There were many problems with the situation I found myself in, but the main problem was how much I liked it.

Dear gods. I was in trouble.

"This isn't what friends do," I whispered.

"Oh?" Cernunnos mused. His arm tightened around my waist. "We aren't doing anything untoward." The *yet* he didn't say hung in the air between us.

He gently tugged on the back of my hair, tilting my face up. His eyes burned as he gazed down at me. "Desire hums through your body. I've felt it since the moment we met. You burn with need all the time, and I know those desires have gone unfulfilled for well over a year."

He had no idea how long I'd been unfulfilled. "I am not sure what's happening here."

Cernunnos smiled. "You are denying your very nature, Moira. More than a vampire, more than a fae, more than a magical experiment, you are different than anything or anyone I've ever known. You've weakened yourself in your fear."

I tried to step away, but his arm was locked around me like a vise of iron. "Cernunnos."

"Taste me again."

I blinked. "No." I could smell the blood running like ambrosia through his veins. He was too close, wrapped around me like sunshine in the morning, and his proximity was messing with my head.

I put both my hands against his chest and tried to push away. It was like pushing against a brick wall. He bent his head and nuzzled the space between my neck and shoulder, inhaling my scent. "I feel your hunger." He smiled against my skin. "Both of them."

Heat flooded my cheeks. "I am not going to bite you."

"Why not?"

"Because we're not in a life-or-death situation!"

He pressed a hot kiss against my throat. "I'm well aware."

A small moan escaped me. "That's untoward," I gasped.

"Bite me, Moira."

His hands slid under my tank top, hot against my skin.

"You could have asked me this when we were on different seats."

His dark chuckle shivered over me. "Where's the fun in that?"

"You could have any woman." I sucked in a breath as his thumbs stroked down my ribcage.

"And you could have any man."

I snorted. "Cernunnos."

"Moira."

He pressed light kisses up my throat. "Take my blood. Consider it a favor to me. I want to test a theory."

"Then what's all the kissing for?"

"Just a bonus." He bent down and scooped me in his arms. "I'll tuck you in."

A huff of laughter escaped me. "I'm sorry I hurt you last time." Knowing I could have dulled his pain, made my bite something to look forward to but didn't have time for, still bothered me.

"You were in a hurry. And I have an extremely high tolerance for pain."

Our faces were so close I could kiss him. And trust me, I thought about it.

Cernunnos was smoking hot.

"I can make it not hurt," I said quietly.

Cernunnos smiled and walked me to my bedroom. "So that's a yes?"

I wouldn't agree to anything right now. "Let's do it in the morning," I lied. "I don't want to be up all night."

He frowned but when he saw I wasn't going to budge, finally nodded. "Fine. First thing when we wake up."

My eyebrows went up. "We?"

"Mm hmm. I already told you I'm staying here."

"On the couch?"

Cernunnos's wicked chuckle sent a tremble of excitement shivering down my spine.

Yep. I was in trouble.

I woke up drooling, splayed on a powerful golden chest. Muscled arms dusted with golden hair wrapped around me, and the steady rise of Cernunnos's chest made me realize this was real.

I was in bed with Evie's dad.

But even more weird?

All we did was snuggle last night.

I blinked a few times to get the sleep out of my eyes, my mind whirring as I tried to figure out exactly how we'd gotten into this situation. When he woke up, he was going to make me bite him. Or at least heavily encourage me to do so.

The thought of it was not unpleasant. I was in too much of a hurry to revel in his taste the first time, but Cernunnos was delicious.

Was he right about my energy levels being linked to my consumption of human blood? I'd grown much thinner than normal over the last few years, so his theory held weight. I consumed a lot more blood before I met Evie, but I still had the fatigue.

Cernunnos was right. I'd compensated for it.

"I can almost hear your spiraling thoughts," Cernunnos's deep voice rumbled.

His arms tightened around me when I made to roll away. "Nope. We're not getting out of bed until we seal our agreement."

"What's the experiment?"

"I want to feed you every few days."

I froze. "What."

He chuckled. "Every few days, Moira. I want to see the effects of my blood on your energy levels and your weight."

"You calling me skinny?" I couldn't even be mad. I was.

His lips thinned in disapproval at my flippant attitude. "I'm saying you're underweight and undernourished."

He flipped me over in an expert move I never saw coming. All I got out was a squeak of alarm before I was underneath him, trapped by his powerful lithe frame. His stunning eyes swirled with power. "Now. Bite me."

I let out a scared little laugh. "I don't think you've thought this through."

"What is there to think through? I feed you. We see if it helps. If it does, then you know to switch your food sources and the frequency of how much blood you consume."

I stared at him. "And what if it's not any of that but the source I'm feeding from?"

It took him a second to realize what I was saying. "Ah." A contemplative look stole over his face. "You believe my blood is different from any others you could consume."

"I don't believe it. I know it. You're a god. I didn't have your blood long enough to experience any real effects other than some lingering powers. If I feed from you frequently, who's to say I won't get addicted?"

"Has a vampire ever been addicted to blood?"

"I don't know much about vampires. I'm not exactly a typical one, and showing my face around their kind seems foolish." My kind wasn't exactly plentiful in the areas I'd lived in, though I suspected Emberwood Falls had its fair share. Vamps tended to keep to themselves, and everyone else liked it that way considering their nutritional requirements.

I was known around the area. It helped that I hadn't dragged anyone into an alleyway to bite them.

"My theory stands. If you show any tendency toward addiction, we'll stop, and I'll purge every bit of my blood from your body."

"What if your blood is the only thing that helps my weight or my energy?"

His lips twitched. "Will you come up with something else once I refute this question? Over and over again for eternity?"

He still loomed above me. "Do you perhaps need some proper motivation?"

I sighed. "This seems like a bad idea."

"Because you feel bad, Moira. Not because you don't want to."

"Dammit, Cernunnos." I did not want him to be right.

He dipped his head and brushed his lips across mine. I went still.

"That seems like a bad idea, too."

He coaxed my lips open. "I can satisfy your other hunger, too. The one you've waited so long to quench."

When he kissed me the second time, there was nothing gentle in his touch. Sparks burst behind my eyes when his tongue swept over mine. Magic bloomed in the air, soft and sultry against my skin. He smelled of wild and ancient things.

My hands roamed over the smooth skin of his back as I met his demand, pleasure searing my soul.

I had the sense to break away. "This isn't wise."

"Do you need to be wise?" Power swirled in his heavy-lidded eyes.

"I—um."

He kissed me again, this time nudging my legs open so he could settle between them. The evidence of how he felt about our current situation rested against the inside of my thigh.

My goodness. I cleared my throat and tried to unscramble my

brain at the same time. I can't remember the last time I had a man —a real one—in the spot this one was. "I guess we don't need to be, but I don't do casual. Not really. I thought I could, but there's an entire Keep of willing shifters here, and I still haven't done a thing."

I almost did a thing and got caveman carried over Ethan's shoulder when he found me, and that, unfortunately, put most shifters on the Moira is off limits bandwagon. Even if it hadn't, I don't think I would have pulled the trigger on anyone.

Except for Ethan, who wanted me but didn't want the guilt that came with pursuing me. And who I had to let go of. When people told you who they were, you had to believe them.

Even when you didn't want to.

He dropped a kiss on the side of my mouth. "Have you ever done casual?"

I slowly shook my head. There'd never been anyone extremely serious, but I also never ran around throwing my goodies all over the place. Nothing wrong with anyone who did, but I liked commitment. I wanted to come home to someone and snuggle on the couch and know that person wasn't waiting for the next hookup to text before he left me.

"Do you do casual?"

Cernunnos smiled. "Most people are too afraid of me. The power dynamic is always off. I would never be with a lover too frightened to enjoy herself."

His hand slid under my tank top.

"There's a power dynamic here," I breathed, my eyes rolling in the back of my head at his curious fingers.

"Is there?" He slid my shirt up and over my head.

And gods help me, I let him. "You know there is."

"Hmm. If you say so." He toyed with one of my nipples.

"Can you please—I am having trouble concen—"

He replaced his fingers with his mouth. A strangled scream tore from my throat. "*Gods.*"

"Beautiful, Moira." His other hand undid the tie in my joggers.

Would it be so terrible if I enjoyed myself? It had been so long.

He slid up my body, his throat right by my lips just as he slid my pants down. "Let me ease your hunger, both physical and emotional. It doesn't have to be anything you don't want it to be. I am not a jealous man. Take other lovers if you wish. Do whatever you wish. Just let me please you."

I stilled. He said the wrong thing. "I'm a jealous lover. I don't want you to have other lovers. I would never have another. Not while I'm with someone. I'm not…wired that way."

His fingers slid between my folds, teasing the slick, swollen flesh.

All my thoughts scrambled into one giant mess. "Gods." My teeth gritted. "I'm trying to have a conversation with you." The words came out stilted and breathy.

"I'm listening."

I let out a strangled laugh.

"Say yes, Moira. Sink your teeth into me, and I will sink into you. I haven't had a lover in centuries. If you don't want to be with anyone else, then don't be."

"And will you promise the same?"

He lifted his head. "I know you care for another."

His fingers were still doing insane things, and it was difficult to keep up with what he was saying because I was getting close…

"I need you to stop," I breathed.

He slowed, just barely. Which might have been worse. "You care for another," he repeated. "And this is new and beneficial to us both. I cannot promise you forever, not with the way things stand. But I can promise you here and now and the near future. This will end when you love someone else. I will not stand between you if you decide to be with him or anyone else for that matter. But know I will never hurt you intentionally. I will come when you call. I will cherish you during our time together, and I will love you if you let me. You will never wonder where you stand with me. Ever, Moira."

Tears sprang to my eyes. He knew the deepest secrets of my

heart and didn't seem to care. He only wanted me. I had no idea why or what he saw in me that appealed to him more than a nubile fae woman. But he was in my bed, in between my legs, and touching me so skillfully I thought I might explode.

I still couldn't help myself. "And what happens if I fall in love with you?"

"Then I will make you a queen and give you whatever you wish for the rest of our lives."

My fangs grew heavy in my mouth, the potent toxin used to make my bite enjoyable filled to the brim.

Cernunnos's eyes widened. "Moira?"

He snapped his fingers, leaving us both completely naked.

Oh gods.

One of his hands pushed my leg up, opening me to him.

I brought him closer. Poised at my entrance, his powerful body stilled. His throat worked as he waited for my decision. As propositions went, his was an excellent one. Neither of us were virgins, but both of us were choosy. He saw something in me I didn't understand, and I genuinely liked him. It helped that I was hella attracted to him, even against my better judgment.

We were both single. My eyes cast a crimson glow over his face as my vampiric nature came out to say hello. His nostrils flared and he closed his eyes.

"Say the word," he gritted.

I sank my teeth into his neck, pumping that toxin into his bloodstream before I drank. Cernunnos jerked, gripped my hips, and slid home.

Pleasure overwhelmed me. He let out a loud, shuddering moan that almost undid me.

"Fuck," he gritted. "*Moira*. Oh my fucking gods." Cernunnos began to move in powerful strokes, every one bringing me closer and closer to the edge.

He spoke in a language I'd never heard as our combined magic rose through the air, a beautiful tangle of syllables as I drank. I met each thrust of his hips, and when I had my fill of his blood and was about to seal the wounds, he shook his head.

"No," he gritted. "Let the world know you've claimed me."

Release barreled over me, more powerful than I'd ever experienced, a shattering scream ripping from my lips. Cernunnos followed me over, his breath choppy and rough, his entire body shuddering against me.

I lay there too stunned and out of breath to speak.

What in the actual shit?

"Fucking hell, Moira." Cernunnos let out a shaky breath. He was doing his best not to crush me under his weight, but the poor guy didn't seem to have the energy to move. "What the hell is in your bite?"

I blinked. "Umm. Normal vampire stuff?"

He snorted. "Wrong. I've been bitten before. Numb, a little bit of a pleasant sense, then nothing. Your bite is unlike anything I've ever experienced."

I peered up at him. "I'm sorry?"

His chest rumbled with amusement. "Never say you're sorry for that." He managed to roll off me but grabbed me around the waist and pulled me against his body. My back lay against his chest and a heavy arm lay draped over my hip. He pressed a kiss to my shoulder blade.

"I can't believe we did that," I said in a small voice.

"Well." He exhaled. "I'm not even a little sorry. Are you?"

I took stock of myself and realized I felt better than I had in years. My stomach was full, my limbs were sated and lazy, and I could spring out of bed and run a marathon if I wanted.

He chuckled. "I'm right, aren't I? You're already feeling better."

"Don't be smug," I chided. "I can't be sorry for that. We're adults, aren't we?"

"We are," he agreed.

"And we're making no promises to each other."

"I think we've been honest with each other as much as people like you and me can be. I meant every word I said."

I snuggled into his chest. "As did I. Still complicated, though."

"Aye," he said in a thicker accent. "Yes, it is."

"Are we going to tell Evie?"

He snorted against my hair. "The moment you walk out of your apartment, every single shifter in this Keep is going to know what you've been doing. And with whom."

"Oh goodie," I said faintly.

Just in time for someone to bang on the door.

CHAPTER

Twenty~Seven

I rolled away from Cernunnos with a groan and quickly dressed.

"Want some coffee?" I asked.

"Always."

I glanced up at him, and my mouth went dry. He lay golden and muscled and tangled in the sheets. His hair was mussed and his eyes were heavy and sated.

And he was looking at me like he couldn't wait to do it all over again.

Goodness. We'd just entangled ourselves in a complicated web, and I thought maybe I should feel bad, but the guilt didn't come.

Evie wouldn't judge me.

Ethan had shown me he would never give me his heart.

I swallowed hard and nodded. "I'll be right back."

The incessant pounding came again.

"Coming!" I called, smoothing my hair down as I padded to the front door.

I opened it and froze.

Ethan stood outside, holding a bag of my favorite donuts. He opened his mouth, frowned, then snapped it shut.

"Well," he said quietly. "It appears I've interrupted something."

Magic boiled in the air behind me. I shut my eyes as warmth hit my back.

"Hello, Lord," Cernunnos said. To his credit, he sounded a little subdued, not satisfied or gloating.

I craned my head up to glare at him, but Cernunnos wasn't looking at me.

When I looked back at Ethan, his eyes had strayed to the two perfect puncture wounds on the side of the god's throat.

"I see," he said with a nod. A ring of gold encircled his iris. He held out the bag and took a step back.

I would not apologize. I'd all but thrown myself at Ethan only to get soundly rejected each time. "What did you need?"

His golden gaze met mine. A hundred emotions flashed through them, and none of them were anger.

That made me feel worst of all.

Ethan swallowed hard and spoke. "I came to warn you. Your mother has escaped her cell. Our trackers have been unable to locate her."

With a final look at both of us, Ethan turned and walked away.

I closed the door and sagged against the frame. "Shit."

"He would have known. Today, tomorrow, even a week from now. It would make no difference."

"I know."

He nodded and went to the kitchen to start the coffee pot. I took a beat to rearrange my thoughts and padded after him to make a cup of tea.

"You didn't do anything wrong," Cernunnos said as he measured out the grounds.

"I know." Our eyes met. "I don't feel guilty, and I wonder if I should. Mostly I just feel sad."

"It's natural to feel that way when we hurt someone we care about."

"I don't regret what we did."

A smile tipped one side of his lips up. "Good. Neither do I."

"I need to tell Evie."

He flipped the machine on and leaned against the sink. "Would you like me to be there?"

I choked on a laugh. "Absolutely not!"

His chest rumbled with a deep chuckle. "Fair enough."

I sank into one of the kitchen chairs and buried my head in my hands. "Gods. She's going to be horrified."

"You might be surprised. She's been around the fae and shifters for a long time. Her sensibilities are not as tender as they once were."

"I'm not talking about the sex part! I'm talking about you!"

He grinned shamelessly.

"You are the worst," I grumbled.

His grin turned into a full-on belly laugh. "How I enjoy you, Moira. In so many ways."

"Do not ever say that to Evie."

He threw his head back and laughed so hard he started coughing.

"Ass." I got up and poured my cup of tea. While I was at it, I poured him a cup of coffee and slid the mug over.

He snagged me around the waist and pressed a kiss to my hair. There was something so warm and comforting about him, edged with wild violence. It appealed to the predator inside me. I leaned against his chest and sighed. "This is weird."

"Mmm. And good, I hope?"

My heart warmed. "And good."

"And Ethan?"

"He made his choice long ago. I just took too long to listen."

"Remember what I said. I will not stand in your way if you decide he is who you want."

I turned in his arms and lifted my hands to his face. "I am a one-man woman. Regardless of where this goes, I'll never allow anyone else's hands on me."

His eyes swirled. "Perhaps I can learn to be jealous," he mused.

I stood on my tiptoes and dropped a soft kiss on his lips. He deepened it before I could pull away until my knees buckled. Cernunnos caught me and hauled me onto the counter where he kissed me senseless.

"You may not be jealous, but I am," I growled.

He smiled against my lips. "No other will touch me. This I swear."

"You speak like such an old man sometimes," I teased.

There was another knock on the door. I groaned.

Cernunnos grinned. "I'm going to take a shower. You will enjoy this visitor."

He winked and helped me off the counter.

"What does that mean?"

He didn't answer on his way to the back, just flashed me another grin.

Gods, he was sexy.

I answered the door to see Rowan and Evie standing there. The Lord's eyes widened within seconds, undoubtedly smelling Cernunnos and me all over the apartment.

Evie elbowed her way in and made her way into the living room. "You've been holed up here way longer than normal. Is everything okay?"

She stopped and turned, her eyes widening. "Oh. My. Gods."

My cheeks went crimson.

Rowan let out a low laugh as Evie cursed and dug in her front pocket. She pulled out a wadded up bill and slapped it into Rowan's outstretched palm.

"Told ya so," he said with a shit-eating grin.

It took me a minute. "What the hell? You were betting on me?"

Evie flopped onto my couch. She had the grace to look sheepish. "I almost won," she grumbled. "You couldn't wait one more week?"

I let out a horrified laugh. "Et tu, Brute?"

Evie shrugged. "Sorry. Dad's been watching you like a hawk for a while now, and you haven't dated anyone in years. I'm his daughter, but I'm not blind."

I sank onto the couch and glared at her. "How much did you bet?"

"I owe Rowan fifty bucks. That was just a down payment."

Rowan tucked the money in his pocket. "I take other forms of payment."

He winked at Evie.

"Gross."

Rowan leaned against the wall and crossed his arms. "After what you two just got up to, you think I'm gross?" He rolled his eyes. "Hypocrite."

Evie covered her mouth with her hand, but her eyes were sparkling.

"We need ground rules," I grumbled.

"I agree." Evie nodded. "We will never, ever discuss your sex life."

"Done." I mimed a zipping motion.

"Second, if you and Dad get married, I will never, ever call you Mom."

Rowan choked.

I tapped my chin and pretended to think about it.

"Moira!"

"What about Stepmonster?"

Evie blew out a breath. "Don't be an ass."

"Relax. Your father and I have an understanding."

She held up both hands and gagged. "Do not say another word." Evie rose. "Is he here right now?"

"Shower's on," Rowan said helpfully.

Evie closed her eyes. "Gross. Alright. This is going to take some time to process."

When she opened her eyes, they shimmered with tears. "On the other hand, I'm glad if you're glad. I'm happy you found someone, even if it's temporary. Or mutually beneficial."

She grimaced, making me laugh. Evie reached for me and brought me in for a tight hug. Her floral scent washed over me. "We saw Ethan," she whispered in my ear. "Everything okay?"

I nodded. "I gave him what he asked for."

Evie sucked in a breath. "Maybe not in the way he wanted."

"Yeah," I agreed. "Regardless. It's done."

She squeezed me a little tighter. "I'm sorry."

"I'm good with my decisions, Evie."

And as I hugged my best friend, I realized for the first time in a long time, I was telling the truth.

"We need to talk later, when this stuff with Soren is over." I pulled back, letting her see by my expression how serious I was.

She nodded slowly. "Alright. Wine and cheese night?"

"Definitely."

Evie brushed a kiss over my cheek and tucked a strand of hair behind my ear. "Say the word, and I'll be there." She smiled. "You look better. Healthier." Evie nodded decisively. "I like you this way."

My cheeks heated. "Get out of here before things get weird."

Evie rolled her eyes. "Call me."

She hurried out of the apartment just as Cernunnos came out of the bedroom wearing nothing but a towel.

Our eyes met. I wiggled my eyebrows and used every bit of my vampiric speed to tackle him.

CHAPTER

Twenty~Eight

ETHAN

eers around a campfire were becoming a regular thing for us.

"I fucked up." Admitting it pissed me off. But I had, and he was the only one I felt comfortable admitting it to. I'm not sure how Rowan and I had become friends. He and I had little in common except for the insane women we cared about, but here we were.

Having beers in the middle of nowhere while I bitched about what a fuck up I was.

"Yeah," Rowan agreed.

I let out a disgruntled snort. "Asshole."

Rowan crossed an ankle over his knee. "I agreed because I've been in a remarkably similar situation."

"It's not the same," I growled.

"Nothing is exactly the same. But I cared about a woman very much and didn't step in when I could to keep her from stepping into the arms of another man." He took a sip of his beer. "And I spent the next year watching him treat her like absolute shit and couldn't do a single thing to stop it."

"He's obviously not treating her like shit." And that made everything worse.

Moira looked healthy. Happy. She'd gained enough weight to fill out the hollows in her cheeks and erase the shadows under her eyes. She spoke more, talked more, and Cernunnos wasn't even around her all the time.

It was making me insane.

Three weeks had passed since I knocked on her door and smelled the evidence in the air. It took everything I had not to launch myself at him and tear off his face.

The only thing to stop me was the knowledge that Moira had given me exactly what I asked for. She stopped giving too much of herself when I wouldn't give her anything of me, and someone else stepped in and offered her what I couldn't.

"She's not in love with him," Rowan said.

My attention snapped to him. "What."

Rowan sighed and set his beer on the ground. "It's only been three weeks. Moira has been single for years. She's never been the kind to rush into anything, and a relationship with the former fae king is one she'll be wary of for a while. Not to mention he's her best friend's dad. I'm not saying it won't happen. Things are rolling in that direction, but right now, without giving too much away, they like each other. A lot."

"That doesn't make me feel much better."

"It means you're in a better situation than I was," Rowan grumbled. "There's still time."

There really wasn't. "Nothing has changed for me. I'm still the same man I was when she told me to get the hell out of her house. She deserves everything but I have nothing to give."

Rowan nodded. "Then it seems like you're shit out of luck."

"Thanks, friend," I said dryly.

Rowan shrugged. "Look man. You can be pissed off all you want, but Moira did nothing wrong. She's an adult in an adult relationship that's going well. As much as I hate to admit this, because I don't care for Evie's dad all that much, he's good to her. Moira is thriving around him. As far as I'm concerned, she did the right thing. She deserves more than you're giving her. If you want her, you have to take the steps to be the man she needs. If you aren't willing to do that, you need to let her go."

In the past I might have lunged across the fire and choked the younger Lord, even knowing he was right. Time and wisdom had mellowed the hell out of me. Make no mistake. I still wanted to choke him, but only because I was mad at myself. "Easier said than done."

"You can still be her friend. Moira doesn't have enough of those. But you can't push her boundaries. Not now and not anymore. One thing Moira has always been is loyal to the bone. If you press her too much, you'll lose her completely."

I tipped my beer up and finished it. "Not sure I can do it."

"You know what you need to do. Either way, you'll make the right decision."

I sat there staring into the fire long after Rowan had packed up his chair and walked home.

Twenty~Nine

The last time I talked to Soren was my response to his, YOU BITCH text after we left him to handle the oncoming spell cloud alone.

Saying he was less than enthused to see me was an understatement.

"Hi ya." I sat on his porch enjoying a cup of lemonade his sexy Second had given me.

"What do you want?" Soren was looking decidedly less sexy than normal. Dark shadows had taken up residence under his eyes, and he'd lost weight. "I'd ask how you got in, but I smell Evie around here."

Having the fae queen as a bestie came in handy sometimes. Plus, this was her land and her wards. She could walk through any meager protection Soren might be able to create for himself. Not that he had. He was still relying on everyone else to fix the problems he'd made for himself.

"The witches still on your tail?"

Soren glared at me. "I'm sure they'll be back soon."

"You sure? It's been a few weeks. Maybe they've given up." They hadn't. Evie and I caught wind of them on our way in.

Mom wasn't with them. She'd taken off to parts unknown, but

I wasn't foolish enough to believe she was gone for good. Mom was a snake in the grass waiting for her prey. She'd be back soon, I had no doubt.

Soren plopped down in the other chair and reached out to snatch my glass away. He took a long sip and sighed. "They sent a black cloud of death after me. I doubt they've given up after that kind of effort."

"Well look at you and your magic penis driving witches to insanity."

Soren leaned his head back and closed his eyes. "Moira. Can you stop? Please?"

The poor bastard sounded defeated. "I'm here to help you finish the witches off."

His attention snapped to me. "Seriously?"

"Why else would I be here?"

"I dunno," Soren said, giving me the side eye. "To rub salt in the wound? Maybe put a tracking device on me so the witches can locate me 24/7?"

I clicked my tongue. "Oh ye of little faith. They tried to kill you. Several of us witnessed the attempted murder. We couldn't very well exterminate them without true just cause. So I got an official document allowing us to kill them with just cause."

Soren blinked. "Excuse me?"

I dug in my purse and waved the paper at him. "The Lords, minus you, convened and authorized us to use lethal force."

"We never needed a piece of paper to put someone down before."

"It's a brand new world out there, Soren. And all this was kind of your fault. No one really blamed the witches for wanting to kill you."

Soren let out a laugh. "You really are worse than Evie."

I reached over and patted his thigh. "Yes, but the difference is the Lords like me, and I'm good at my job. Now we have a fancy piece of paper giving us permission to wipe out their entire coven."

"How'd you get it?"

"Sending a black cloud of death at a Lord tends to annoy even the grumpiest of leaders. Once we notified the witch leaders or whatever the hell they're called and threatened to reexamine their territory boundaries, they were more than happy to authorize the lethal force." I smiled sweetly at him. "You're welcome."

"That paper is all well and good, but it won't help us get through their wards."

"Evie and Cernunnos are coming back as soon as we get your okay."

Soren frowned. "My okay?"

"Yes. Aren't you the Lord of this temporary land?"

A faint smile crossed his lips. "Sure doesn't feel like it, but I suppose I am."

"Then let's go kill some witches. Cool?"

He scrubbed a hand through his hair and slowly nodded. "It's true then, isn't it?"

I stole the lemonade back. "Is what true?"

"You and the god."

I still wasn't comfortable talking about whatever this was I had with Cernunnos.

"I smell him all over you."

I grimaced. "Living with shifters is not awesome."

He grinned. "You look good, Moira. Really good. Whatever this is, it agrees with you."

I never thought about how I looked in the past. Immortality tends to make any tendency toward vanity slowly fade away if you weren't in the spotlight all the time. But Soren was right. I was a child when turned and became a slender, almost skinny adult as a result of Mom's experimentation. Gaining weight had always been an issue. It turned out I was accidentally starving myself. I needed blood far more often than I thought, but it wasn't human blood that fortified me.

I needed magical blood. How I'd deal with that if Cernunnos and I didn't work out was something I couldn't think about right now. He'd been happily feeding me, and we were slowly going further between feedings to see if I could keep my weight and energy levels up.

So far, we were up to five days with no ill effects.

I liked Cernunnos. A lot. He was funny and weird and sexy, and he'd given me something fae almost never gave up. Blood was hoarded because it contained power, and he'd given me his because he thought I may need it.

Even if things didn't work out, I would always be grateful to him.

"Thanks," I said finally. "I feel really good." And my powers were...

Well. I no longer believed I was much of a vampire, that's for sure. I was far more than a creature who drank blood to survive.

He slid a curious look my way. "And Ethan?"

Unsurprisingly, he'd heard the rumors. He was a Lord. "We're both professionals and can work with each other when we need to."

Never mind that Ethan did all his communication via email and text these days. I'd smelled him on Keep property, but he'd kept a wide berth from me. While his absence saddened me, maybe it was for the best.

I cherished Ethan's friendship, but things had always been complicated between us. With the promise I made Cernunnos, I intended to be very careful in any future dealings with the Lord.

Soren grunted. "I'm surprised Ethan's taking this so well. He's level headed, but he's a shifter. We all knew he was more possessive of you than he should be."

"Ethan and I are, to quote my favorite show, *workplace proximity associates*. That's all."

The edges of his eyes crinkled with amusement. "Sure, Moira. Keep telling yourself that."

He took the lemonade back and finished it off. "For what it's worth, I realize I was a complete asshat to you." He paused and winced. "To many people. All I can do is apologize and try to be a better person."

"You've already apologized. We're good, Soren. As long as you survive the witches, you'll get your second chance to make amends."

Soren cracked a laugh. "Always so uplifting and motivational, Moira. Can't wait to see your show on the road."

I winked and stood. "Half-price tickets for you because you need it the most."

"Ass." Soren rose and stretched. "Want to call your people? I'll send for Seth."

I texted Evie and summoned Cernunnos mentally. Now that we were closer, I could feel his presence around almost all the time, even when we weren't together. Weird.

As an afterthought, I texted Ari and let her know what we were doing. Mom more than likely had the weapon, but if she popped in while we were getting rid of the coven, Ari might miss her chance to grab it if she wasn't here.

Within seconds, Evie and her dad popped in, followed directly by Ari. Evie gave her an odd glance. The wards were up, and Ari, if she were merely a jeweler, shouldn't be able to bypass Evie's wards.

I met Evie's eyes and shook my head once. We could get into it later.

Evie frowned but nodded. She was still getting used to all the weird things just like I was.

Seth sauntered over, his brows flicking up when he spotted all the women. He dipped his head when he spotted Evie. "Hello, you stunning creation."

Evie snorted. "Glad to see you're still the same, Seth."

He grinned. "I can't go around disappointing my favorite woman, can I?"

When he spotted Ari, his eyes narrowed. "Another fae? We really are going hunting, aren't we?"

Soren jogged inside and came back a few minutes later with a backpack. "Water and some food in case we get stuck out there for longer than planned."

"Let's hope not," Evie said. "I can't stand dealing with witches. If I get stuck out here, I'm going to get cranky."

"No one wants that," I assured them all.

Evie gently shoved me. "You should see what happens when Moira gets cranky. Worlds will fall."

Ari nodded to Evie. "Nice to see you again, Lady."

"I'm surprised to see you here. Is there something I should know?"

"Later," Ari promised her, after a quick glance at me. "I may need to renegotiate the terms of my move."

Meaning Rowan didn't know who the hell she was either, and she was living in Emberwood under false pretenses. Most Lords would kick her out upon finding out who she really was, but Rowan was understanding of people hiding their true origins as his wife had done the same thing for years. If Ari had done nothing wrong, Rowan would have no quarrel with her.

Time would tell, I guess.

"Soren can't get through their wards. I'm hoping our fae friends today can take those down while we come in from the back." I nodded at Cernunnos, who was staring at me with intense scrutiny.

We'd met up this morning for some fun times, but from the look in his eyes, that might not have been enough.

Heat touched my cheeks. "We do not need to take prisoners. Our license authorizes us to use lethal force on every witch we find." I paused. "No children, even if they're witches."

"There's a pregnant witch there," Soren added.

"Take her into custody. The no children rule applies to anyone pregnant as well. We'll figure out what to do with them once we handle all the other witches. If you're not good with what we're about to do, leave now and no one will say a word. If you hesitate when we get there, I will not allow you back on any other missions."

Missions seemed like the wrong word considering I was just a rando vampire about to clean out a witch coven, instead of a commando with an assault rifle about to take down a world leader, but the witches had proven both deadly and dangerous.

Which reminded me, I'd forgotten to tell Soren something. "As a result of Soren's extracurricular activities—"

Soren winced and turned beet red.

"Dating witches has been strictly prohibited without first raising the possibility to the junior council."

Soren sputtered. "I wasn't *dating* any of them."

"Perhaps that was the problem," Cernunnos drawled.

Evie coughed to cover her laugh.

"Witches are known to be problematic and prone to violence at the slightest provocation," I went on. "And though the Lords express their regret at having to maintain such a measure, it will prevent something like this from happening in the future."

They'd made me memorize that little tidbit. I didn't like them dictating who someone could or could not date, but this had turned out to be a far bigger mess than any of us anticipated. We couldn't keep wiping out covens every time one of the Lords or any other shifter got tangled up in a few.

Unfortunately for everyone involved, witches often acted as one when one of their own was slighted. They rarely handled problems without consulting their coven mates. This almost always escalated matters into much bigger problems than some-times necessary.

I didn't think we should be taking them out like this because Soren couldn't keep it in his pants. But Soren was a Lord and was therefore considered more important because of some rare set of skills I had yet to witness from him.

But here we were. I was the lackey performing necessary duties.

Duties I hoped I wouldn't have to keep doing very soon.

"This seems like a leap in logic," Evie said.

"Shifters and witches don't really mix," Seth said. "I can see why they might institute such a rule."

"They don't have to mix," Cernunnos said. "Soren wasn't looking to mix, only for a brief respite away from his worries."

Soren stared at the god. "Do you have a problem with me?"

"Not all, young Lord. Merely a concern for your lack of discernment."

Evie put her hand on Cernunnos's arm. "Dad."

Seth grinned broadly and leaned toward Soren. "He's saying you're a hoe."

I had to cover my mouth this time.

"I'm well aware what he's implying," Soren growled. "Gods. Can we get this over with so I can go back to ignoring the lot of you?"

"They're on Ethan's land," Seth said. "Do we have permission to enter his territory?"

"We do." He sent me a text early this morning with his approval, though he hadn't said whether he'd be there or not.

We could always use an extra set of hands when tangling with witches, but with Cernunnos there, it might be better if he stayed behind.

"Cernunnos and Evie will act as transporters. Ari?"

She nodded. "Happy to take whoever needs a ride."

"Anyone bringing any weapons?" Seth asked.

Ari patted the small leather bag at her side. "I have what I need."

Cernunnos and Evie shook their heads. Soren had nothing. I had a few bottles in my crossbody I could use if things got dicey, but no guns or knives or anything like that. I've found I didn't really need them.

Seth pulled out a massive knife strapped to his back. I'd totally missed the harness or whatever he was wearing. "You could cut the head off a grown man with that thing," I mused.

He grinned. "Or a full grown witch."

Evie snorted. "Alrighty then. Let's maybe save the big ass

knife for the real feisty ones." She raised one of her feet. "These are new shoes. I'm going to be annoyed if I ruin them because you're indiscriminately beheading people."

She and Seth shared a scary grin.

I waved my phone. "I'm sending you all the pinned location. We'll drop in half a mile away and walk the rest of the distance. There's one witch who should not be there, but if she is, you must take all caution to avoid her. Don't get hit by any of her spells. If you see her, go the opposite direction."

Everyone stared at me. "Does she not belong to the coven?" Evie asked.

"She's the hired help. That black cloud from a few weeks ago probably belonged to her, drawn from her power and the extra juice from the coven. Do not take her appearance for granted. A pretty witch is just as deadly as a mage."

"What I'm hearing is do not engage with the stunningly pretty witch." Seth wiggled his eyebrows.

"I'm serious. If you see her, and I don't, call out to me. I'll back you up."

Evie was watching me closer than anyone else. She stepped over and took me by the elbow. "Moira and I will follow. See you in a bit." Cernunnos grabbed Soren. Ari grabbed Seth.

Evie didn't budge. "Spill it," she demanded. "Who's the witch you're so scared of?"

"I'll tell you everything later," I promised.

"You'll tell me some now."

"My mother."

Evie sucked in a breath. "She's—"

My BFF never took long to figure something out. "Ah. Is this similar to me and Cliona?"

"A little," I admitted. "But mine isn't doing a thing to protect me and never has."

"If I can kill her, should I?"

Another thing I loved about Evie. She would not hesitate to take someone out if they hurt someone she loved.

"Cernunnos tried and failed."

Evie's brows climbed high on her forehead. "How," she demanded in a flat voice.

"We have to go."

She stubbornly crossed her arms and refused to move.

"Fine," I growled. "Ari's a famous fae weapons master. Mom somehow came into the possession of a god killing star thing. Something. I don't really know. She almost took him out with it. So, no. Please don't try to kill her. Not until we know she doesn't have the star anymore."

Evie tightened her grip around my arm. "You and I are going to sit down with a shit ton of cheese and wine when this is all over. You've been keeping secrets."

"Yes, well," I said with a sigh, "looks like it's your turn to worry about me, isn't it?"

A flash of hurt appeared in her eyes before she swept me away.

CHAPTER
Thirty

Ethan stood next to Soren. His face went blank when he saw us pop in, and he turned away.

Hurt flickered in my stomach, but I shouldn't have expected more. I'd wounded Ethan, and a wounded animal never responded well to the one who'd harmed them.

Magic saturated the air, none of it belonging to any of us. The witches were close.

We hunkered down in a dense wooded area. Having Evie here was a boon.

"Can you see what's going on in their camp?" I asked quietly.

Evie nodded and kicked off her shoes, settling onto the ground a moment later. She stuck her fingers and toes into the ground and closed her eyes. A sweet floral scent rose in the air a moment later as her magic rose.

Soren watched her for a moment. "It's always weird to watch her do that."

A vine snapped up from the ground and slapped him in the back of the knee, making him lose his balance.

Ari let out a bark of laughter.

"She's gotten a lot better with her magic," I said mildly. "Evie can hear everything we're saying right now."

"And respond," Evie said dryly, her eyes still closed tight.

Cernunnos stood by himself. I walked over to him. "Hey."

He didn't reach out and draw me closer. Neither one of us were really wired that way. His eyes warmed when he spoke to me, and that was enough. "Something isn't right."

Cernunnos watched the area ahead. Nothing seemed amiss to me, but it was hard to tell with all the magic floating around us.

"Do you think she's there?"

"Difficult to say. If she is, she's not using her magic." Cernunnos's lips thinned. "Probably to give us a false sense of comfort if she is."

His gaze went to Ethan. "I'm sorry he is so angry at you."

I glanced at the other Lord. He was handsome as usual, the gray streaks at his temples more silver than normal in the evening light. Today he wore a flannel shirt and old jeans. His boots were scuffed and worn, and he looked like we'd dragged him from outdoor chores. I rarely saw him like this.

Ethan wore a lot of suits and slacks. I liked him either way, but this rugged and casual look suited him.

"I don't think he's angry at me," I whispered. "He's angry at himself."

Cernunnos's eyes flickered. "A self-aware Lord. Those tend to be rare."

"Eventually, they come around. Things are still raw. Maybe in a few more weeks, he'll thaw a little. We still have to work together, so he can't freeze me out forever. And to be fair, he doesn't ignore me when I contact him for work issues."

Cernunnos's swirling eyes caught mine. "How are you feeling?"

I smiled. "You know I'm feeling good. Why are you asking?"

"Just checking. We're on day five. Need a top up?"

I shook my head. "I feel just as good today as I did the first day."

He took a step into my personal space, his voice dropping

lower. "Maybe we could temporarily halt the experiment, and you can take a sip anyway."

I grinned up at him. "You'll mess all your calculations up, Doctor."

"Hmm. Could be worth it."

I swatted at him. "After this first go round, we'll know exactly how long I can go. Then we can have all the fun we want. Deal?"

"You run a tight ship, Moira. I suppose I have to agree."

"Good."

I turned just as Evie's eyes were opening. "We have a problem."

"Of course we do," I muttered. "What is it this time? Have all the gods congregated in one place to show us who's boss?"

"No," Evie said. "Every single witch in the coven, besides one outlier, is pregnant."

No one said a word for a long moment, before I, eloquent as always, spoke. "Um. What?"

As one, we all turned to look at Soren.

He held up his hands and backed up. "What. No! I swear to you I did not sleep with all those women."

"Again," Cernunnos said mildly.

We were all still staring at him. What kind of reputation did you have to have for none of us to be overly surprised by Soren knocking up an entire coven who had tried to kill him at least twice?

Soren swore and scrubbed his hand over his face. "I swear to you. I did not touch those women. Not after all that!"

I wasn't sure what to think. Ethan stepped up. "Lords don't harm children. We call this off immediately. One of us will act as a representative and warn them off of Soren. If they return, they'll sign their death warrant."

"Are you sure, Evie?"

She made a little wave at herself. "I'm the new Mother Earth, so yeah. I'd know if someone was really pregnant."

"Could you sense anything about the infant?"

Evie blinked. "I didn't try. They'd sense my presence if I had."

"Well shit." I felt bamboozled. "It's only been a few weeks. How did they all get knocked up at the same time?"

"When a man loves a woman..." Seth drawled.

"You think it's one guy? What if they had some sort of ritual?" This was blowing my mind.

"Some witches use sex magic to enhance their magic," Cernunnos said. "Maybe this was how they got the cloud to work."

Soren's nose wrinkled.

"Don't look so grossed out," I chided. "You're no better."

The Lord sighed. "Can we just stop with all the teasing on this. Yes, I have many notches on my bedpost—"

"Your bedpost looks like rats got ahold of it and had a chewing contest," Seth drawled.

Soren shot him a dark look. "You're supposed to be my Second," he growled.

"Oh I am. I'll die for you, but having to do it because you can't control your pants snake is pretty embarrassing. How will I ever face my friends?" Seth's smile was far too innocent for the devilry shining in his eyes.

"Regardless, they're pregnant now, so their magic won't be as potent, right?" I asked.

"Not necessarily," Cernunnos said. "Pregnancy can make witches even more powerful, if they don't care about drawing from their infant's life force."

I stared at him. "Witches actually do that?"

"They can. Some do. I don't peg this coven as particularly caring of another's needs."

"I'll go as a representative," I said.

"I'll come with you," Ethan said.

My mouth opened to deny him, but we were on his land. "I— okay."

I touched Cernunnos's arm. "We'll be back in a little while."

"How will we know if you're in trouble?" He didn't seem

concerned. We'd been practicing a little with my magic. We both know I should have no trouble taking on a coven.

Ethan patted his back pocket. "I brought a flare gun. We're in the wilds out here and sometimes we need them. The ground is moist enough to prevent a fire, so it should be safe to use."

Evie waved. "And you have me. I'll monitor wherever it lands."

He dipped his head in thanks. "Ready to go?"

With him? Absolutely not.

CHAPTER
Thirty-One

Ethan was walking way slower than he should be. I slowed my steps to walk beside him.

"Everything okay?"

He let out a short laugh.

"Right. Dumb question. We should hurry up and get this done so we can call everyone if we need to. They'll get nervous if we take too long."

I sped to a normal pace.

"Moira."

I thought about speeding up more, but that would make me look petty. I was only petty to people who deserved it. No matter what Ethan had done, I still cared about him.

"This is probably not the time to discuss personal business." But I slowed my steps and waited for him to catch up.

What he said next surprised me.

"Are you happy?"

I glanced over. He looked straight ahead. His hands were in his pockets and his posture straight. If I didn't know him better, I would think he was merely checking on a friend, but there was a nuance to his question.

"Cernunnos treats me well." There was more to it, though. "At this point in my life, he gives me what I need. Whether that lasts forever, I can't answer."

He nodded. "You look good. Healthier. I—I'm happy for you."

I grinned and let out a chuckle. "Liar."

Ethan huffed a laugh. "Yeah." He hesitated. "Listen. I don't want it to be this way between us. You were well within your rights to do what you did. I haven't been the most demonstrative man, and I've gone about things all wrong."

"I don't want things to be weird between us either. But I can't go back to how we were. It isn't fair to any of us."

"Us including Cernunnos now?"

"Don't poke the bear."

His chuckle this time was less forced. Ethan reached out and took my elbow, stopping me. I could have pulled away if I wanted to, but I waited.

He looked down at the ground for a moment before lifting his eyes to meet mine. I always thought his eyes were so stunning. So dark they seemed black in certain lights, when they were really one of the deepest blues I'd ever seen. "I'd like us to start over."

He seemed sincere. And steady. Ethan wasn't barking orders or demanding I do something. In fact, he was downright reasonable.

And that made me awfully suspicious.

"Are you alright?"

Ethan snorted. "Someone wiser than me rightly schooled me on my most recent behavior concerning you. I took some time to look inside, and I realized the bastard was right."

"So no popping up inside my house at all hours of the night?"

"Not even a little."

"None of you getting jealous when someone makes eyes at me?"

His jaw clenched. "If I do, I will do my best to ensure you do not know about it."

I almost laughed, but he was being so sincere, I swallowed my amusement down. "And you will treat Cernunnos with respect?"

"I always have." His eyes were glittering with gold flecks now, telling me I'd pushed as far as was wise.

"Fine." I stuck out my hand. "My name is Moira. You know my best friend, Evie."

Ethan stared at my hand for a long moment before he took it in his larger one. His skin was far warmer than mine would ever be, callouses dotting his palms. He worked outside so much, even the immortal blood inside him had given up on healing them. "Ethan Flint. It's a pleasure to make your acquaintance."

In the past, he would have held on too long, made some double-edged quip meant to knock me off kilter. He did none of that today. While he held on a beat too long, Ethan let go far sooner than normal and took a step back. "I hope we see each other again, Moira."

I grinned. "Me too, Lord."

His eyes glowed. "Please. Call me Ethan."

"Such familiarity for a first meeting," I teased.

The tension broken, Ethan jerked his head. "Come on. Let's go convince some witches we don't want to kill them."

"But we kinda do."

"Yes. Well. They don't need to know that."

We smiled at each other and kept walking.

The witches' new digs looked much the same as the other. Several multi-person tents, a main fire pit and smaller fires dotted the area. The witches milled around, some carrying buckets, others holding greens or herbs in their hands. All of them were stunning in their own way. Soren might be a horny old bastard, but he had good taste.

"If I didn't know them, I'd say they look downright peaceful today," Ethan murmured.

"Be on your guard for my mother," I warned.

The witches couldn't see us yet, and the wards would prevent them from scenting us unless one of us used magic.

Ethan let out a deep exhale. "I know we haven't talked, and

I'm sorry for that. Your mother should not have been able to escape. None of us can figure out how she managed it."

"She's always been tricky," I allowed. "Someone didn't frisk her properly. It's the only explanation."

"You think she swallowed something or..." His voice trailed off.

"Did a good impression of a drug mule?"

Ethan's expression made me chuckle. "Or that," he said.

"I wouldn't put anything past her. You got an x-ray machine at the Keep?"

He slid a glance my way to see if I was kidding but scratched his head when he realized I was completely serious. "Err. Guess we could buy one, but I don't think she's going to come willingly this time."

"She didn't come willingly last time, either. But you're right. She'll be twice as hard to take down the second time."

"You up for this if it comes to a fight?" He eyed me in the way one warrior does to another. "As much as I hate to admit this, you look better. Stronger." His eyes narrowed. "Your magic feels different to me."

I wasn't sure how much to tell him. Anything I said would hurt him. "I've been experimenting with my magic and my food intake."

Ethan turned his head to study me. "Food." His gaze slid down my body and back up to my face. "You've gained weight and muscle." Realization settled over his handsome features. "Blood, Moira? Have you not been consuming enough to fuel your body?"

"Ahh..." I scratched my face. "It's a long story."

He exhaled softly. "I wondered, you know. Everyone said you were a vampire, and I could feel that part of you, but there was always something else lingering there. Your blood intake was never as much as it should have been, even with someone of mixed blood."

His jaw tightened. "Cernunnos figured it out."

"He did."

"Well." He fell silent for a moment. "I should be grateful to him then for helping you see what you're capable of."

I slapped the back of my hand against his forehead to check for a fever.

"Ass," Ethan chuckled. He squeezed my hand. "I'm serious. Whatever he's helping you with, it's working. You've always been beautiful."

My heart began to thud.

"Now you glow from the inside out."

Ethan released my hand. "Ready to get this over with?"

I cleared my throat. "Yes. Let's go."

Ethan walked ahead, and I stared at his back. I felt like I was in a new emotional minefield and had no idea where to step.

Shaking the feeling off, I hurried after him.

The witches spotted us when we were about twenty feet from the wards. No sign of my mother. She'd make her entrance at the worst possible time, I was sure.

The witch Soren spoke with last time greeted us. "We did what your god asked and left his land."

"It's Evie's land. Not his."

She rolled her eyes. "Whatever. We left. Why are you here?"

"You sent a death spell after Soren while you were on Lord Ethan's land."

Ethan had turned on his full Lord visage. Eyes glowing a strange molten gold flecked with midnight blue, he stepped up. "We have no wish to fight, but your reckless disregard for life has put us at odds."

"Your Lord," the witch hissed, "doesn't deserve to be in power if he treats women like he treated us!"

To my surprise, Ethan inclined his head. "Perhaps. We assure you we will investigate his actions later."

Oh shit.

"For now, I am here to tell you to move on."

Magic pricked at the back of my neck. Dread pooled in my

stomach. Something was out there watching us, and I didn't think who or whatever it was lurked behind the wards.

I turned and scanned the horizon. Ethan's territory was mountainous, and he lived in a heavily forested area. The witches weren't far from his Keep. Lots of hiding spots around us.

Maybe we should have brought Evie. I couldn't sense whose magic it was. They were too far away. A quick count revealed all the witches left from the coven.

I tapped Ethan's forearm. He didn't visibly react, the twitch in his forearm muscles the only tell he understood my message.

The witch's face turned sour. "We just got here."

"Then you shouldn't have tried to kill one of my own, witch."

The same dark-haired witch from before made her way through. She stopped a foot away from the wards and inclined her head. "Lord. Thank you for allowing us the use of your territory."

"I'm afraid I'm here about that," Ethan said, not sounding apologetic at all.

"Ah." The witch's smile was thin. "You wish us to vacate once more."

"As you've tried repeatedly to kill one of the Lords, I'm afraid my safety is now in question."

The witch smiled. "I can assure you we never target anyone who hasn't targeted us. You are perfectly safe around us."

She sounded so sugary sweet I almost believed her.

The wards fell and a dozen spells flew from all the witch's fingers.

CHAPTER
Thirty-Two

He'd be furious at me later, but Ethan wouldn't be able to handle getting hit by more than one of those spells. Using all the strength I had, I shoved Ethan, sending him flying through the air.

He landed with a thud and a grunt just as the first spell hit me. Ethan rolled, his face furious when he lifted it from the ground.

Our eyes met. Searing pain bloomed in my chest.

The second spell hit me. I went to one knee.

"MOIRA!" Ethan scrambled to his feet.

The third spell hit. Blood bubbled from my lips. My insides felt like they were rearranging themselves. One of the witches laughed.

I slammed my hands against the ground and called Cernunnos's magic. Power sizzled in my veins, the warm, ancient feel of his magic sliding from my fingertips. The earth buckled, sending the witches flying into the air. A blur of gray fur flew past me and slammed into the leader. Blood sprayed in an arc.

I crawled toward him, the spells working to slow my heartbeat. Three death curses.

They were waiting for us.

Blood dripped from my nose and eyes, plopping to the ground

in large droplets. I reached for that strange power I'd been given at Caelan's Keep, opening up a portal and pulling out anything that might be able to help me.

Cernunnos thought I might be able to use the power with my will, as in I pushed an image into my mind and opened the portal holding that image. A silver spear appeared in my hand.

"Fuck," I whispered and choked. I was a vampire, not a Viking.

The spear warmed in my hand, and I used it to help myself to my feet. Ethan had taken three witches down and was trying to reach a fourth, but there were still several witches still on their feet throwing spells. Fortunately, death spells took a lot of prep, and they were tapped out on that front.

He'd shifted and couldn't use the flare gun. My eyes went to the pile of his clothing. It had to be there. Leaving him felt like a betrayal, but if I could summon help, we might make it out of this alive.

I thought of Cernunnos. We were somehow linked these days, through either our shared magic or something more concerning, and all I could hope was he would hear me.

I used the spear as a cane and sort of half loped, half dragged myself to that pile. I went to my knees when I reached it and dug through until my fingers hit hard metal.

"Thank the gods." I coughed up a concerning amount of blood and raised the gun in the air, firing off a flare.

I stabbed the spear into the ground once more and forced myself into a standing position.

When I lifted my eyes, my mother stood before me.

Her green gaze studied me, more solemn than I'd ever seen her. "You're dying."

I coughed up blood. "I'm aware," I wheezed.

"That does not suit my purposes."

I let out a rasping laugh. "Can't say I care."

She raised her hand to cast a spell.

"No!" I threw magic, but I was too weak to send more than a trickle that Mom easily dodged.

"You're too weak," Mom mused. "Though I'm curious how you are using god magic."

She stepped closer and gripped my chin, forcing me to meet her eyes. "Curious. It seems all those years did something other than allow you to age. Tell me, Moira. What secrets are you hiding from me?"

Warmth bloomed in my chest, Fee's presence making herself known. If I died, so would the rest of the phoenix's spirit, and that was a shame after what she'd done for Evie and the world.

I smacked my mother's hand from my skin. "Don't touch me." I wheezed.

She laughed. "Still far too hardheaded for your own good."

I looked over her shoulder, hoping against all hope Evie and everyone else would show up, but no one was there.

A pained yelp rang out from the witch's camp. Hopelessness filled me.

"If you're looking for your friends, I'm afraid they have been delayed." She smiled, the sight sending terror through my veins.

Every time she smiled like that, she delivered pain. I shuffled back, a moan of agony bubbling from my throat. Everything hurt. Every breath I took felt like inhaling razor blades.

Mom stepped forward. "If you don't allow me to help you, you'll be dead in a few minutes."

"Going with you is worse."

"Who says I will hurt you?"

"You always hurt me."

Mom shook her head. "I needed you to be something more than you were, so I molded you into what I needed." She made a tsking noise. "And then you ran from me before you knew why I needed you."

"To keep your smooth skin and lustrous hair," I growled. "You wanted my essence because you're obsessed with immortality."

Mom shook her head. "It's not quite that simple, my darling."

"I don't care." The next step back was easier to take, that warmth in my chest blooming into a full glow.

I rested most of my weight on the spear. "Leave now and you won't die."

My mom's laugh sounded like silver bells. It always creeped me out how someone so evil could have such a beautiful laugh. "Oh, Moira. It's such a joy to see you all grown up."

Another yelp. I had to get to Ethan. Hanging on this long was a miracle. A Lord could do many things, but going up against an entire coven would test even their mettle.

I took another step back, pretending to try to hobble away. Fee's power burned through my veins, the witch's curse slowly fading. Mom came closer, a satisfied smile on her lips.

She always expected to win.

My hand tightened around the cool metal. I planted my feet on the ground and watched her.

"You look like you're making your last stand. Really, Moira. There's no need to be afraid of me."

An incredulous laugh broke from me. "You broke every bone in my body! You poked and prodded me with fire." My voice trembled. "You hurt me. Every single day. And not only that, you brought in a vampire to turn me against my will when I hadn't even gone through puberty. You wanted me to stay forever young so you could continue hurting me."

Mom stopped. Her eyes narrowed, perfect lips shaping into a sneer. "You owe your life to me. I gave you everything!"

"I never asked to be born! You only wanted me because you wanted to consume me. Don't act like you were in any way charitable."

Mom shook her head, tears filling her eyes. "You have no idea what it's like to be me. How hard it was back then for a woman alone with a child."

"I don't *care*," I hissed. "I would have been better off if you smashed my head in with a rock the moment I was born!"

Mom sucked in a breath. "Moira! You were my most prized possession."

Her eyes flickered as she realized what she said. I slowly lifted the spear from the ground.

"Possession," I repeated. "That's exactly what I was to you."

She took a step forward. "Moira. Mothers make mistakes."

I stared at her incredulously. "A mistake is forgetting to send the signed folder back in Kindergarten. Or forgetting to make cupcakes for a bake sale. Not letting a creature do unspeakable things to your daughter."

All the horror and rage rose up inside me. I let Mom come closer, her hands outstretched as if she actually cared about me. She always pretended to care about me when she wanted something, and whatever she wanted must be important for her to expend the power to distract Evie and the others and come at me. She was a few feet away, tears spilling down her perfect cheeks.

I lifted the spear and hefted it at her.

Mom's eyes went wide as the spear hit her in the center of her chest, sinking in with a sickening squelch and a flash of strange purplish magic. Too concerned about Ethan to worry about it, I left her there as she swayed in shock and ran to Ethan.

Fee's magic still worked to expunge the curse, and I was running at about half speed, but I was up and I was still alive.

That had to count for something.

CHAPTER
Thirty-Three

Two witches still stood. Ethan's fur was covered in blood and gore, his back leg obviously broken. I threw my hand up again, hoping for something to help me. Something cold landed in my hand. I glanced down.

An ornate silver dagger humming with faint magic. Alright. Weird, and I didn't expect to be in hand to hand combat with a witch, but the day was still young.

I tucked it into my back belt loop and kept running. But something occurred to me. The world had just handed me a fancy dagger, and I was running toward two bitches trying to kill Ethan.

I drew the dagger once more, aimed, and sent it flying.

A short scream and the one on the right went down. Not dead but disabled for now.

Ethan didn't look behind him. Smart guy.

Underneath my feet, the earth rumbled. A sob threatened as two familiar strains of magic shattered through the air. Vines sprang from the ground, wrapped around the last witch's ankle and flung her into the air.

"Ethan!" I yelled.

The wolf turned slowly. His eyes were full of molten gold. Saliva and blood dripped from his maw. I went to my knees, hissing at the residual pain in my bones, and raised my hands to Ethan.

His golden eyes softened. He took a single shaky step toward me, his entire body trembling.

"Help is here," I said quietly. "We'll get you home and to your healers as soon as we tie up loose ends."

He was going to be fine. I repeated the words in my head, over and over like a mantra.

Ethan let out a huff and collapsed.

I let out a shriek of alarm and scrambled over to him, running my fingers through his matted fur. Ethan's body was littered with cuts and wounds. I sucked in a hissing breath when I found one particularly deep cut, blood oozing from his ribs.

"You're going to be okay." I pressed my hand gently against the ruff of his neck and bent close.

Ethan's breaths came in shallow rasps. A flash of light cracked in the air as Ethan transformed.

"Moira," he whispered.

"Help is coming, Ethan. Evie and Soren and Cernunnos are here. They're going to help."

"Too late." A sad smile.

"Nope." My chest burned, power rising within me.

Ethan lifted a hand and touched my face. "I'm so sorry."

"Don't say that shit to me when you're dying, asshole."

Ethan let out a pained laugh, followed by a wet cough.

He slow blinked. "Don't give Soren my territory."

"No one but you is getting your territory."

"You are the most beautiful thing I've ever seen, darling." Ethan's eyes fluttered closed.

I ran my hand down his ribcage, feeling amongst the fur and blood and gore for his heartbeat, only to find a terrible silence.

"No." Tears slid down my face. "No!"

I pressed a hand to my chest. "Fee. If you ever wanted to help, now's your chance. Please."

A rainbow of colors burst from my fingertips telling me two things:

Fee heard me.

And Ethan was dead.

I pressed my fingers to Ethan's skin. Prismatic light bloomed over his body as Fee's magic worked to revive him. I whispered a prayer to the universe and lay down beside him, ensuring my hands stayed in contact with his body.

A hand rested on my shoulder. "Hey," Evie said. She lay down beside me and curled her arms around me. "You cool going into the ground if need be?"

"As long as it brings him back."

Evie brought up a cage of vines over our bodies. "I'll wait with you until we know for sure."

I nodded. Her cool fingers brushed through my hair as we waited.

"Is Cernunnos outside?" I asked.

"He is. Dad felt when Ethan…passed."

"He can't be dead."

"When Rowan died, it felt like someone had torn my heart out with their bare hands. A mating bond is different from what you two have, but I know there's a bond there. I can feel it. We all can."

"Is it a mating bond?"

She hesitated for a moment. "No. Not yet."

Tears spilled down my cheeks. "He doesn't want it."

"I know, Moira. You two live far enough away to keep one from triggering. I'm not sure that's any consolation, but the distance will keep things at bay."

"He loves someone so much he never wants to move on. Can you imagine what that must be like?"

"I know what it's like," Evie said softly. "Every time I see Rowan, I see my heart living outside my chest."

"I don't know what that's like. No one has ever loved me that much."

Evie scoffed. "Lies. But I get what you're saying. One day I know you'll feel the same way I do."

I shook my head. "Mating isn't in the cards for me."

"You can't know that."

"I do. I'm happy with the way things are now. Cernunnos and I have a good relationship. He's good for me."

Evie started braiding my hair, her cool fingers scraping against my scalp. "You're good for him, too. Maybe that's enough."

It had to be. "Is my mom dead?"

Her fingers stilled. "We didn't see your mom."

I closed my eyes, resisting the urge to scream bloody murder. "Did you see a silver spear?"

"Ari picked one up. She seemed totally freaked out by it."

"Mom got away." I sighed. "Again. Fuck."

"Not cleanly. She left enough blood behind to supply a hospital."

"Huh. Maybe she died somewhere else."

Evie and I both laughed. Neither of us had ever been so lucky.

The rainbow light died down, the warmth in my chest slowly returning to normal.

Ethan didn't stir.

"Maybe Fee's power only works once," I murmured. "She already resurrected him before. Maybe it doesn't work on the same person again."

"Don't say that. A phoenix's power is never ending, and Fee left it to you. Magic doesn't work only once."

I rubbed my fingers through Ethan's hair and pressed my face against his neck. "Come back to me," I whispered.

Light bloomed in our cage of greenery, casting an iridescent sheen over my skin.

"A heartbeat," Evie said. She gently squeezed my arm. "He's alive."

Evie took the cage down slowly and scooted away. I lay there with Ethan until he opened his eyes.

"Hi," I whispered.

He blinked several times. "Moira," he croaked. "You're alive."

"And so are you." I smiled. "Again."

Ethan closed his eyes and let out a shuddering breath. "How?"

I wasn't ready to tell him about Fee. "Evie helped," was all I said.

He frowned but Ethan was so tired, he didn't question anything. "Your mom?"

"A problem for another day." I touched his cheek and rolled away, slowly coming to my feet.

Cernunnos stood there watching me carefully. I limped over to him and lay my head against his chest. Warm arms encircled me. "My gods, Moira. You are dripping in death magic."

"Yeah," I said on a sigh. "About that. Let's chat about it later."

Ari stomped over, waving the spear at me. "Where the hell did you get this from?"

I pretended innocence. "Umm. The witches had it in their camp."

In her other hand was the dagger. "And this?"

I waved my hand at one of the groaning witches. "Same. You might want to check to see what else they're hiding."

Cernunnos chuckled softly. "Ari seems like someone you will eventually grow to trust."

"Today's not that day."

He exhaled. "Only one of the witches was actually pregnant. They managed to trick even Evangeline's senses with a powerful spell. I've never seen anything like this coven. Their magic is disturbing."

"Did anyone die?"

"Four witches. Evie would have been devastated had they actually been with child."

I tilted my face up to see his lips twitch. "Now she's trying to figure out exactly how they did it."

Something had been bothering me about this. "They knew the Lords wouldn't go after them if they were pregnant. Their softness with children is well known."

"They investigated Soren well."

"I don't think it was them. This has my mother's hands all over it."

"You think she was trying to ingratiate herself with the witches to eventually get to the Lords?" He stroked his chin. "Once she made herself useful to the Lords, she might be able to get to you more easily. Both clever and diabolical."

Cernunnos chuckled. "But we screwed that all up didn't we?"

"We certainly did." And thank goodness for that. If I hadn't gotten involved when I had, my mother might have been able to take Soren out, put the blame on the witches, and offer her assistance to the Lords in a ploy to her ultimate goal: put me in chains once more. This time I couldn't hide my shudder of disgust. "I put nothing past that awful woman."

His arms tightened around my waist. "We will find her. And when we do, she will answer for her crimes."

I smiled up at him. "Let's keep letting Soren believe this was all because of his horniness." I looked around. "Where is he anyway?"

"One of the witches popped him with a boil spell. He's completely covered up."

I let out a cackle. "Oh no. Our pretty little Lord isn't so pretty anymore?"

Cernunnos grinned. "That penis isn't getting anywhere near a woman for at least two weeks."

"Serves him right."

"How about I take you home? Ember has been asking about you."

Warmth bloomed in my chest, simple joy this time. Fee rested contentedly deep in my veins.

"I'd like that."

Cernunnos picked me up and carried me away in a gentle gust of silver and emerald wind.

Epilogue

ETHAN

I watched Moira play with the new edition to Rowan's Keep, a joyful small fox she named Ember. The not quite a vampire laughed, her dark hair streaming behind her like a banner as she ran barefoot across the grass.

"She's beautiful, isn't she?" Evie asked.

Rowan was over talking to Declan and Hope. Evie had elected to stay behind for some reason. She and I had never been on the best terms, but the little flower psycho was growing on me.

I nodded, knowing I would never be able to make amends for how I treated Moira when all she wanted was to give me her heart. "How long has the fox been here?"

"Ember pops in and out as he pleases. He used to only come when Cernunnos was around, but when he realized no one was going to eat him, he started coming around more often. Now they're all but inseparable."

"I'm glad she has the company."

Evie glanced over at me. "She's got an entire Keep of people."

"Moira doesn't like to be alone, especially when she's eating."

Evie tilted her head and studied me closely. "You could fix this, you know."

I snorted. "Moira has made her boundaries clear. I'm choosing to respect them."

"As you should," Evie said. "You don't have to violate them to heal the hurt you caused."

"I'm not the man she needs." Why I admitted that I had no idea. Evie proved surprisingly easy to talk to.

"Maybe one day you will be."

I looked at her. "She's dating your father."

"I'm well aware." She reached for the pitcher of iced tea and refilled my glass. "But my father is not her mate, is he?"

Keep reading for a look at Book Eleven
Shifting Allegiance

Shifting Allegiance

BOOK 11, SHIFTER LORDS

After the last job with Soren goes terribly wrong, Moira's list of enemies grows longer by the day.

One of those enemies she shares with Ethan, a Shifter Lord who has haunted Moira's thoughts ever since she spied on him over a year ago. Forced to work together, Moira has to fight her growing fascination with the powerful leader in order to protect her growing found family and her peaceful way of life.

But with a body and mind made for war, Ethan isn't a man who promises peace, and Moira's fascination, as it turns out, goes both ways. This Shifter Lord isn't so easily deterred when he finds something he wants, but when tragedy strikes, and Ethan is the only one who can save her, Moira has to fight against her very nature to keep herself free from entanglements of any kind.

She's always sworn not to get involved, but there's something about these Lords that turns all of Moira's promises right on their head.

But Moira is nothing if not stubborn, and if Ethan wants her, he's going to have to play the long game—a game both of them might lose.

Trailer Park Transylvania

Psychic Cleaner

The Magical Soapmaker Mysteries

The Goddess Chronicles

Vikings of Virginia

The Deadicated Matchmaker

Sheryl likes cake too much and can be found hoarding it while hiding from her children in the pantry closet.

Follow her on Amazon at: https://www.amazon.com/S-E-Babin/e/B00J1J236A

A small press bound by the belief that every voice matters.

Sign up for our newsletter to learn about new releases and more.
https://oliver-heberbooks.com/subscribe/

Follow us on social media:

facebook.com/oliverheberbooks
instagram.com/oliverheberbooks
amazon.com/oliverheberbooks
youtube.com/@OliverHeberBooksPublisher

www.ingramcontent.com/pod-product-compliance
Lightning Source LLC
Chambersburg PA
CBHW020337180726
47991CB00020B/1740